# Taste

# of

# Love

SIFA ASANI GOWON

This edition published in 2015 by Ankara Press

ISBN: 978-978-53151-5-8

# One

Adoo wasn't having a great day. It started with her son, Zander, spilling Milo all over his school uniform, which meant that she had to hurriedly change him, making her even later to join the morning traffic than she already was. She managed to drop him off just in the nick of time and head to town. The go-slow on the road had tasked her old Toyota Tercel clunker – rather unsuitably named Bunny and manufactured in the year 1254 as far as she was concerned. The radiator overheated and the engine stopped. For the second time that week. She had spent the next few hours having the car fixed, trying not to pull her hair out or scream in frustration.

She ended up being late picking Zander up from school – again – earning her the wrath of the teacher on after-school duty. She probably thought Adoo was the most negligent parent ever.

Back in the car, Adoo barely managed to manoeuve her way off the choked freeway to a narrow shortcut to her next destination. It was the middle of April and the expected rain was late in coming. The heat was stifling. Sweat ran down her back, making her blouse damp and melting her make-up. A glance in her rear-view mirror confirmed her fears: her face was a shiny and congealed mess.

Just when she thought things couldn't get any worse,

she found herself at one of the town's trendiest lounges, struggling to keep her calm. Adoo didn't frequent nightclubs or fashionable hot spots because they simply weren't her scene. She was at The Bar-Rage because Aduke, her flatmate and business partner, had asked her to buy a pizza on her way to choir practice.

"Please, please just do this favour for me and I won't ever ask you for anything again," Aduke had begged. *Yeah right,* Adoo thought. Aduke could sell ice to an Eskimo with her charm.

And now here she was, waiting for the snooty upstart of a club hostess to explain why she'd had to wait more than half an hour for one measly pizza. Instead, 'Miss Priss' was on the phone with someone – a man, judging by her coy looks and simpering little girl whine – and ignoring her. Adoo wasn't one to judge, but couldn't she take her private business somewhere else? Zander had fallen asleep on their way to the club and she had parked Bunny under the shade of a large eucalyptus tree, leaving him asleep in the car with the windows down. She tipped the guard on duty in the large compound to keep an eye on him. She didn't know how long the boy would stay asleep with the heat outside and she wanted to be in and out as soon as possible.

"Look ..." she said, inwardly counting to ten in a bid to control her rising temper. "I'm sure that is a very important and life-altering phone call but could it wait? I've got a kid asleep in the car and I really need to get going, as I am already running late. This hasn't been the greatest of days so I'd appreciate it if you would just—"

"Lady," the lady retorted. "Can't you see I'm busy?" Adoo raised her eyebrows, inhaling slowly. She drew herself up to her full 5ft 2, adjusted her glasses and released all her pent-up frustration.

*** 

Toby was immersed in financial reports, expenses and other miscellaneous matters when he heard a knock on his door. He was beginning to nurse a pulsing headache at his temples – whether from stress or his lack of sleep, he was unsure. He looked up irritably, wondering who was disturbing him. He had made it clear that, unless it was an emergency, he did not want to bothered.

"What is it?"

His tone was clipped. One of the newer employees popped his head around the door, an apprehensive look on his face. Toby glowered at him and he shrank back.

"Ehm … sir? There is a problem and … sir …" he stuttered. Toby sighed. *Can't they do anything without me?*

"What kind of problem could there possibly be that cannot be fixed without me?"

"Well … sir, it's Emem … and there is a woman shouting … the other customers … ehm … even the security is …"

"If you can't stop tripping over your words then I guess

I'll have to go and see for myself," he said, rising up from his desk.

As he walked around his desk he asked himself again why he had accepted this job as a club manager in Jos, of all places in Nigeria. The weather and scenery were wonderful, and the people pleasant but … he was a big-city boy at heart so why come to this quiet yet disaster-prone area? The pay was good, that was for sure, and he had to admit that Jos provided the perfect opportunity to bury himself in work and escape Abuja and all the memories.

He heard the fracas before he saw it. As he reached the balcony overlooking the foyer, he could see it was Emem, one of the club's hostesses, and a female customer. Emem did her job well but, being good-looking and arrogant to boot, she had a knack for rubbing some of the female clientele up the wrong way. And now he would have to douse the fire she had started. He gritted his teeth and walked downstairs.

***

Adoo was on a roll and the hostess with the 'Emem' badge was the target of her rage. "In case you don't know, you're not doing me any favours. It's my money I'm spending here and I have the right to demand why my order is taking so long. All you have to do is answer and be polite about it!"

"Madam," Emem rolled her eyes and drawled, "I am going to call security to …"

The threat only served to further enrage Adoo. "Call them and see!" she shouted, cutting the hostess off. "If anyone lays a hand on me in this place I swear to you I will remix your face in a way that will win me a DJ award."

"It can't be worse than what we are looking at now," the hostess retorted, looking at Adoo with utter contempt, before pursing her lips and hissing. Adoo stepped forward menacingly, the marble counter the only thing stopping her from launching a physical attack. At this point one of the waiters stepped in to try to defuse the situation, speaking to both women in a placating tone.

"Eh … abeg, take am easy," he murmured to the hostess through clenched teeth, before turning and speaking to Adoo. "Please, madam, exercise patience and—"

"The only thing I am going to exercise here is my hands if I get to where she is," Adoo said, pointing her finger at the hostess. "How dare you speak to me so rudely? Who do you think you are? You think because you are fine you can treat people this way?"

"Madam, maybe you can sit down and try and relax," the waiter said, holding his hands up in a calming motion and then gesturing towards a stool near the counter. Adoo sighed and shrugged, preparing to sit down. Then Emem spoke.

"Maybe we should try and find a smaller chair so that you can reach it," she said to Adoo with false sweetness and a fake smile on her face.

Adoo closed her eyes and tried to dampen the rage in her, aware that creating a scene would not serve any purpose. *I will not slap her, I will not slap her,* she repeated as a mantra in her head. Then she opened her eyes and pasted a smile on her face, grinding her teeth together, convinced that she looked like a shark in the process.

In as mature and polished a manner as she could muster, she said: "I am a professional and I expect, when I walk into a place that prides itself on service and hospitality, to be treated with courtesy. If you spent as much time talking to your customers as you do making private phone calls, you might understand a fraction of what I'm talking about."

"Look," the hostess waved her off dismissively, "I don't have time to waste on you today so go and ..."

Adoo saw red and, putting her hands on the counter, she attempted to launch herself over it and get at the hostess. The waiter who had earlier tried to calm the situation hastily beckoned to a security officer who rushed forward to stop her. But he halted, his hands outstretched, when she turned her enraged eyes on him. She continued to try and jump the high counter, cursing her small stature as she did.

"When I'm finished with you I'm going to speak to your manager and ..."

"That won't be necessary, ma'am." Adoo jumped in surprise as she spun around. She almost smacked into a broad, cotton-shirt-clad chest and she looked up into a handsome imperious face. She had to stop herself from letting out a low whistle of appreciation. He had dark, piercing almond-shaped eyes that lent him an Asiatic look. His lips were full and well shaped with a neat goatee skimming his jawline; his skin was a cross between milk chocolate and amber, like finely brewed Earl Grey tea. His hair was cropped close to his head, not a strand out of place. He was handsome enough to easily give any top male model a run for his money. *God is truly an artistic genius,* she thought. She opened her mouth to say something, but what came out was not quite what she had in mind.

"… Ehm … you shouldn't sneak up on people like that."

"I didn't sneak up on you, ma'am. You simply didn't hear me walk up behind you as you were rather busy … er … explaining matters to Emem here."

Adoo felt heat rise up her face and she was sure her glasses would soon steam up. *Now you've gone and disgraced yourself in front of Denzel Club-ington here,* she thought. She bit her lip and stole a look around. Some of the patrons were chuckling, others staring at her in open curiosity – Nigerian voyeurism at its best. She was grateful that there weren't many people as it was still too early for the night crawlers. And that was just as well as she had embarrassed herself enough.

The security officer who had made the attempt to defuse

the situation looked at the man sheepishly and something in the man's eyes made him slink back to his post.

The man turned his attention back to Adoo. "Ma'am, if you would kindly step into my office I am sure we can sort things out." Then he beckoned to the waiter who had earlier tried to placate Adoo. "John, please escort Miss …or is it Mrs?"

"Ehm … Adoo Ibi … Miss … yeah … that's my name." *Oh, Lord, Adoo, you sound more and more like a lunatic with each passing second.*

"Yes, please escort Miss Ibi to my office," he said as he turned his gaze to Emem. She shrank under his withering stare. "See me afterwards, Emem," he murmured. The coldness in his tone nearly froze Adoo where she stood and she almost began to feel sorry for the hostess. With that, Toby turned around and walked towards his office with Adoo in tow.

# Two

Toby had never understood how such pint-sized women could cause so much havoc. Miss Adoo Ibi couldn't be more than 5 feet tall but he could swear every inch of her carried a punch. He'd had to stop himself from chuckling as he had watched her trying to vault over the counter at Emem, especially when he saw Emem's stricken face.

He invited Adoo to sit down and she did, looking around her and taking things in. Toby took his time sitting down, looking over his irate customer to get a quick profile that would give him an idea on how to handle her.

She was a 'Miss', therefore there was no equally irate husband to deal with, which was a good start. She was also casually dressed in slacks and a loose-fitting buttoned blouse, making him guess that she would be somewhat liberal. As he sat down, he examined her face, which was framed by loose thick braids and creased with a rather embarrassed expression. Limpid kohl-rimmed eyes looked straight at him, magnified by an understated pair of glasses perched on a snub nose. The smooth, chocolate-like skin on her face reminded him of some of the glazed ceramics he had seen on display somewhere. She wrung her hands lightly in a gesture of nervousness.

Toby snapped out of his appreciative reverie, switched mental gears and fell back into his managerial role. "So, Miss Ibi, what seems to be the problem?" he said, in his most customer-friendly voice. She exhaled and pursed her lips before she spoke.

***

"Well … first of all I'm sorry for causing such a scene—"

"It's all right …"

"I've had one heck of a day and she just annoyed me—"

"Perfectly understandable …"

"And when she was rude I just lost my cool—"

"Evidently."

Adoo stopped talking and stared at him frankly. He probably thought she was crazy and was obviously trying his best to defuse the situation. She had an inkling he would be very skilled at calming down irate women. *I mean, who wouldn't calm down after looking at him?* Adoo chided herself for even going there. Men were the very last thing on her mind, no matter how *'Denzel-ish'* they happened to look.

"Look, I know it doesn't seem like a big deal, but it's taking so long for my pizza to arrive. I'm running late for church and—"

"I apologise, Miss Ibi. I assure you that your order will be here in 5 minutes … on the house, of course."

"Thank you, sir."

"And I would also like to apologise for Emem's rather poor attitude in handling your complaint. I assure you it will not happen again. We at The Bar-Rage pride ourselves on giving the very best to our patrons and I would hate for you to have the wrong impression," he said, smiling. The smile never quite reached his eyes though. Adoo nodded. She wanted to be out of there as fast as possible. The proximity to this painfully polite, handsome stranger had her nerves jangling.

"Just to ensure that we keep your patronage, we would like you to have a 50 per cent voucher for the next time you place an order," he continued.

"Oh?" She was taken aback by the offer and the piercing look in those brown eyes.

He smiled and held out his hand, murmuring pleasantries and nodding as she distractedly took it, still smarting from her encounter with the hostess. She was so taken in by his charm that it wasn't until he said an amiable 'bye' to her that she realised that she had walked out of The Bar-Rage with a pizza in her hand and a bemused look on her face.

Miraculously, Zander was still asleep when she got to the car and even Bunny cooperated, starting up as soon as she turned the key. Soon enough, she was heading to church, berating herself all the way. She wished she hadn't made such a fuss. And, to make matters worse, she had lost her cool in front of such a gorgeous guy.

\*\*\*

Toby had gone through the necessary motions, doing damage control. He knew that many people in managerial positions would consider it unnecessary to placate a single customer but he never believed in doing things by halves. One customer was just as important as the next.

As he had talked he had cast furtive glances at Adoo Ibi. She was actually rather cute … in an unconventional sort of way, he supposed. He noticed a small stud in her nose, and, though Toby wasn't a fan of facial jewellery, he thought, rather surprisingly, that it looked quite nice on her. She had an intelligent look about her, one that spoke of grit and character. And she wasn't a pushover, as she had earlier proven. Something about her look, her stance reminded him of Hannani.

The memories came back in a flash and he was transported to a time, four years back in Abuja, when a woman with 'grit and character' had dealt him a blow he wasn't sure he would ever recover from.

After showing off her shiny engagement ring to their friends, Hannani got up and excused herself to use the restroom. Toby knew this would be his only chance to get her alone and speak to her. He had to, if only to regain some measure of sanity. He waited a few minutes before getting up and excusing himself. He carefully avoided her fiancé's eyes as he did, feigning nonchalance.

He rounded the corner to where the restrooms were, out of the sight of diners, and waited until he spotted Hannani coming out of the ladies' room. Her eyes widened as she saw him and she tried to get around him, but he reached out and grasped her arm firmly.

"Let go of my arm, Toby," she said, looking straight ahead, her voice measured and calm. He guessed she wasn't as calm as she seemed, if the hammering pulse at the base of her neck was any indication.

"We need to talk," he said.

"We have nothing to talk about."

"Oh yes we do. You and I both know we never really faced the issue after that day …"

"That … 'issue' is dead and I have moved on," she said, her voice dripping with contempt. "It's over."

"No it's not, Hannani," he said softly. "It's not over. You and I both know we both felt something and it was more than a casual fling…"

Toby shook himself, surprised at the strength of the memory. He had not been serious about any woman since the fiasco with Hannani. Some wounds were just too deep to heal in a hurry. And he was in no hurry.

He was immensely relieved when John came in with Miss Ibi's pizza box. She picked up the package, the steaming contents giving off a mouthwatering aroma and after a flurry of 'thank yous' she was gone. She had begun to make him uncomfortable, sitting across from him and giving him that frank stare. He shook his head, trying to get the image of her eyes out of his mind, and resumed reading the financial reports.

***

"Mommy, I want sweet …"

Adoo cringed, unsure if she was more irritated at Zander's request or his nasal whining. She answered, almost on autopilot. "It's not 'Mummy, I want sweet,' it's 'Mummy, may I please have some sweets?' and the answer is no. I got pizza and I'm sure Auntie Aduke wouldn't mind you having a slice."

The piping-hot pizza in the back seat spread a tantalising aroma through the car as Adoo drove, but her suggestion fell on deaf ears; Zander was resolute in his desire for sweets.

"No, don't want pee-sha! I want sweet," Zander whined. "Mummy! Mummmeeee …" At this point Adoo zoned out, preferring to shut out the whining than respond.

Zander's tantrum would cool down soon enough and she would give him a slice and reward herself with a piece too; too bad for Aduke. That would be one bright spot in her otherwise horrible day. She cursed her bad temper again. *Yep, this temper thing is definitely going on my prayer list.*

The traffic was a little lighter as they headed to church where Adoo had choir practice. She bit her lip, feeling guilty that Zander would have to wait until after practice to go home. She would have to make it up to him somehow, maybe an outing to the zoo over the weekend. His voice had faded as he was distracted by the cars outside. He strained his neck to look out the window, pulling against the straps of his car seat.

The traffic warden motioned for cars in her lane to stop and give way, and she took the opportunity to turn and steal a glance at Zander's profile. His round cheeks showed that, at three, he was still growing out of the 'baby fat'. His thick hair and chocolate skin were Adoo's and his long lashes and well-formed lips were his father's. There were moments in the midst of his petulance that he looked remarkably like his father. Adoo just shook her head.

A hoot behind her brought her back to reality and she put the car in gear, moving forward.

*** 

Adoo walked into the church building with Zander running ahead of her, zigzagging in between the pews. Adoo called out to him, almost losing her balance in the process. She was struggling to carry his bag of spare clothing and snacks, the pizza and her large bag all at once; she was rescued by Aduke Balogun, her flatmate and the pro bono church accountant, who took Zander's bag from her.

"Let me guess: Bunny messed you up again," Aduke said, clucking sympathetically.

"Babe, you don't know the half of it," Adoo said, shaking her head. "It's been one thing after another, a real lesson in patience, which of all the fruits of the Spirit, I have a very low supply of, by the way."

"My pizza fa?" Aduke asked. "I hope you didn't forget

it." Almost immediately an image of Mr Handsome Club Manager flashed through Adoo's mind and she had to shake her head to free her mind of him.

"I don bring am," she said, thrusting the box at her friend. "And I hope you don't choke on it …"

"Haba, choke ke?" Aduke laughed. "Did you have a hard time getting it?"

Adoo then proceeded to narrate the events at the club, ending with Handsome Manager's intervention. Aduke sighed, an exaggerated 'lovestruck' expression on her face and Adoo looked at her in confusion.

"Wetin do you? Why do you have that silly look on your face?"

"Ah-ah? You meet a handsome stranger who swoops in to save the day and you don't think it's romantic?"

"Romantic, ke? I said he helped me get the pizza quickly; he didn't ask for my hand in marriage. Anyway, it was on the house so I'm keeping a piece for Zander as my commission."

"Oh, warreva. I still think it's romantic." Aduke shook her hand dismissively. "Besides, I've heard about the guy, the manager at The Bar-Rage. Young chap, gorgeous, from Kogi - Igbira or Idoma, I think. Toby something."

Adoo stared at her friend in amazement. Where on earth did Aduke get all her information? Some underground gossip network? She didn't even go to nightclubs! Adoo hadn't even thought to ask the man's name.

"How do you know so much about him?" she asked,

with false nonchalance. She was unwilling to admit to Aduke that she actually wanted to know more about this enigmatic Toby something-or-other. Aduke laughed and wiggled her eyebrows.

"Adoo, unlike you, some of us are actually on the lookout for young eligible men. In fact, I will even admit that some of us have fasted and prayed for Mr Oh-so-Right sef. Besides, Jos is a small town so gist goes around; everybody knows somebody who knows something about somebody else."

Adoo shrugged, pretending she didn't care. "Eh OK, then why don't you go and get your own pizza next time? Then you can shout at Emem and Mr Toby can come and sweep *you* off your feet."

Aduke grinned. "That might not be a bad idea." Adoo shook her head with a smile and changed the subject.

"Hmm, my dear, we better get moving. I have to finish up with the choir practice and get on home as soon as possible. I've got loads of flowers waiting to be cut and moulded for that wedding cake next weekend. Looks like I'm going to be on night duty today."

# Three

It was almost 10pm when Toby finally left the club. He hadn't realised just how much time had passed. He had been there since the previous night at the insistence of some of his regular and high-spending friends-cum-customers. He was sorely in need of sleep. The guard mumbled a greeting as he came out and he soon found himself on the road to his house in Rayfield.

The roads were deserted with only a few military checkpoints, a necessary fixture in Jos due to the civil unrest that frequently plagued the city. Toby rolled down his window as the cool night air caressed his face, soft music playing in the background. He had everything he needed in life: he was 34 and running the most popular (and most profitable) hang-out in Jos, which came with a hefty pay cheque and nifty lodgings. Despite his proximity to the constant energy of the nightlife at the club he found that he preferred to spend his free time – when he had it – at home watching the news or reading.

He had had a few casual relationships over the past few years but nothing he had invested in deeply. His erratic schedule usually put a lot of strain on his relationships and eventually the woman would just fade away. It worked well enough for him. Clean and surgical was how he liked it; no mess on either side.

The DJ on the radio warbled some incoherent

commentary and then a Trey Songz song came on, 'Can't be Friends'. Toby hissed softly, wondering how one song could bring back all the memories he would rather keep in the recesses of his mind.

They couldn't just be friends.

"What we felt?" Hannani turned to him. "What would you know about feelings, Toby, given that you don't have a heart? What happened that afternoon was something I will regret for the rest of my life."

Toby felt a sliver of pain slice through him at her words but he said nothing.

"What upsets you more, Toby? The fact that you didn't get to be the one doing the discarding? Or is it the fact that you saw that I can be as casual about you as you have always been with others?"

"Hannani, we did this together. And I don't believe that it was as 'casual' as you'd like to make it seem."

Toby harrumphed loudly, bringing himself back to the present and wondering at his train of thought, blaming Mr Trey and his song for his introspective mood. He quickly switched to the CD player and smiled as a happier, less soul-searching song came on.

The estate generator was working as he drove into his section of the estate, its low rumble vibrating in the distance. Toby remembered that he hadn't eaten much all day and chided himself for not sending someone to buy groceries for him during the day. *Well, I guess it's Indomie and eggs for you,* he thought as he tossed his keys on the dining table and went upstairs to change.

A few minutes later, as he put his makeshift meal on the stove to cook, he thought back over the day's events. It had been a normal day except for Miss Adoo Ibi, of course. He chuckled as he remembered what a punch she packed in her deceptively diminutive frame – small but mighty. He had seen quite a few scenes between women in his life, having caused a few himself, but nothing quite like this. Had it not been for his intervention, the woman just might have succeeded in launching herself right across the counter at Emem!

Toby wondered why he remembered every detail of her appearance. It wasn't as though she was exceptionally good-looking. He had seen more striking women. But for some reason this particular woman had made quite an impression on him. Was it her eyes, full of expression? Her Cupid's bow lips? Or the little cartoon-like nose? Cute yes, but not the type he would normally go for. But then Hannani had not been conventionally beautiful either. She had ruined his ability to merely look at the surface of a woman. Maybe it was because something in Miss Adoo Ibi was so much like Hannani that he couldn't help zooming in on it. But what it was exactly, he didn't know.

He shook his head. *Get a grip, guy. It's just another day, another woman, another customer.* With that he proceeded to eat his rather unremarkable meal.

About two weeks after Adoo's near fracas at The Bar-Rage, she had reason again to curse Bunny. The car decided to have a flat tyre, an hour before a follow-up meeting with a bride-to-be regarding finishing touches to her cake. Adoo stomped out of the car, banging the door, and then proceeded to kick the offending tyre repeatedly, knifing the air with a few choice words. Adoo was grateful that Mary, the bride-to-be, was unusually patient and that the meeting was not urgent. Motorists passed by, unfazed by the woman throwing a tantrum on the roadside. After a few minutes Adoo set to work changing the tyre, muttering a prayer for the preservation of her sanity, while continuing to hope that she would be able to afford a new car soon.

She hummed one of the songs they had practised in choir a few days before as she worked and her calm returned. By the time she had securely fastened the last nuts, her shirt, which had been crisp and white when she started, was stained with smudge marks and her hands were covered in greasy grime. Not a good sight for her meeting with Mary. How could she drive her little clunker back to her flat in Rantya, change and still make it back to town in time? Bunny could barely hit 60 kilometres per hour without violent convulsions. She released a long sigh.

"You changed the tyre yourself. I'm impressed."

Adoo jumped up in fright, dropping her spanner. She

turned to face Toby who was standing less than a foot away, arms crossed with a slight smile playing at his lips. His eyes were a bit bleary, as though he hadn't slept well, but he was looking dapper in a cotton shirt and jeans. She tipped her head to the side, giving him a sardonic look.

"Sneaking up again, eh? How come you always show up after I get into trouble and not before?" she said. He laughed and shook his head. She saw that he was even more attractive when he laughed, with his eyes twinkling and his teeth even. *Goodness, does the man have any physical imperfections at all?* she wondered.

"I don't know. But then you seem to be handling yourself just fine, I think. Not many ladies know how to change a tyre."

Adoo squared her shoulders and tossed her chin up. "I am not most ladies and I can't afford to be a damsel in distress. I can change a tyre and the oil, wash the car—"

Toby laughed again, his hands in front of him in mock surrender. "OK, OK, I get it. You are woman, hear you roar. What a man can do, a woman can do better, abi?"

"No, not like that. I just don't … I don't depend on anyone except myself and God, that's all."

She noticed him raise his brows lightly, and in a flash wondered if she had appeared unnecessarily defensive. It wasn't as though the man had been disrespectful to her. Then he spoke.

"Um … are you going somewhere now?" he asked. Adoo was surprised he would ask and shrugged in defeat.

"There's a client I'm supposed to meet but ...' She gestured at the car and then at her ruined shirt. "Well, this tyre thing has messed me up. I can't go looking like this and Bunny – that's my car – well, she can't take me to Rantya and back in time ..." She let the sentence trail off, embarrassed that she had blurted out her problems to a virtual stranger.

"I can take you back home then, if you'd like."

Adoo looked at him with a mixture of gratitude and fatigue. He spoke again, his tone lighter as though he were attempting to add humour to the situation. "Besides, I don't think, er, Bunny here is in the mood to help you out."

For a moment she considered refusing, so as not to appear to be the overly eager 'damsel in distress', in need of saving. Then, after a few quick calculations that brought her sharply back to reality, she decided to take him up on his offer. *This is certainly not the time for insincere protestations or misplaced pride,* she told herself. She locked Bunny and hopped into his gleaming Mercedes. Inside the car, she leaned back, savouring the luxury.

'Hmmm ... na wa o ... you're really rolling with the bigger boys, aren't you? With A/C sef! I don't think Bunny was even manufactured with an A/C."

"My job does have its benefits, I agree, but it has its downsides too – like staying up till ungodly hours," he said chuckling. "By the way, I'm afraid I didn't get a chance to introduce myself properly. Toby Onoche. Pleased to meet you … again."

"Likewise," she said. There was a moment of silence before he spoke suddenly, as if trying to make conversation.

"So … Miss Ibi, what do you do, besides terrorise club workers, that is?" Adoo scrunched up her nose in shame.

"Oh, it's Adoo, please call me Adoo. Miss Ibi makes me sound like the school principal. I bake and I decorate cakes. You know, for birthdays and weddings, while my friend Aduke plans events and does the decorations. We merged our talents together into one business called Much A 'Do' about Events!

Toby chuckled. "Much A 'Do' about Events! eh? I like the wordplay on Shakespeare and your names."

"You got the wordplay bit? I'm impressed." She laughed.

"Thank you for being impressed, Adoo. So, have you lived in Jos your whole life?"

She shook her head. "No. I moved here a little over three years back."

"Oh, that's about the time I moved here too. Where were you before?"

"Makurdi." The word came out more clipped than she'd meant it to. He only nodded and said no more. She was glad he had decided not to press further.

He reached over to turn on the radio in what must have been a bid to fill the silence with some sort of pleasant noise. The beat and bass from John Legend's 'Quickly' filled the car and Adoo smiled. She looked out of the window as she took in the familiar scenery of Tudun Wada area. Rocky outcrops covered with green grass and vines dotted the scene, with the clear blue sky forming a perfect backdrop. As they passed Hill Station Hotel she cast a furtive glance at Toby out of the corner of her eye, not wanting him to catch her staring.

He was looking straight ahead, concentrating on the road, and his profile was neat and attractive. She couldn't really read much from him, as his face was virtually expressionless. She had no idea why he would go out of his way to help her out, but she wasn't complaining. She didn't like strangers knowing where she lived but here she was, seated next to a stranger, heading to her flat. That was very unlike her.

After they had weaved along the road through Tudun Wada's undulating hillsides, the familiar sights of Rantya loomed ahead with its tightly packed houses and shops lining the front of the settlement. She gave him directions. Adoo's place was located in the area's low-cost housing estate, deep in the settlement, and they had to go along a number of little roads to reach it.

The car pulled up in front of the large, rusty and somewhat dented brick-red gate of her estate. Toby looked over at her and his lips curved into a slight smile.

"We're here, eh? I'll just wait for you while you change." His eyelids looked heavy, as though he was falling asleep and his face was a blank mask – she couldn't guess what he was thinking. She nodded and swallowed, suddenly flustered.

"Er, I live in the last flat with my friend Aduke … and my son." She didn't know why she had chosen to give him that piece of information. It wasn't as though he had asked or even given an indication that he cared.

"Your son?" He raised his eyebrow.

"Yep. I have a three-year-old boy named Zander," she said trying to sound breezy. "He's a terror … but I'm crazy about him. I'll be right back." With that she hopped out of the car and ran into the flat.

***

As Adoo tossed various shirts around and tried to decide what to wear, she thought about the man waiting for her outside. He was an enigma. On the one hand he seemed cold, distant and professional, or at least that was the impression she'd got from their encounter at the club. But then he comes along, offering her a ride and going out of his way to help her out. Maybe he had some sort of "saviour" complex?

And even though he was quite pleasing to the eye she remembered that Teremun had been very handsome too and Zander had been the only good thing to come out of that fiasco. Adoo had learned the hard way to stay clear of the extremely good-looking types as she believed most of them couldn't see beyond themselves. Besides, she had

26

no illusions about her own looks and pretty boys didn't go for ordinary girls like her unless there was something to gain from it. That much Teremun had taught her.

She finally found something acceptable to wear, pulled it on and hurried outside. Toby had a look of wry amusement on his face when she jumped into the car.

"Women," he said, shaking his head and chuckling. "I'll bet you flung around every item you own to find this one outfit. Why is it that you ladies get so … complicated when it comes to clothing and all that stuff?"

"Hey, that's a sexist statement, you know," she said, raising her eyebrows at him as she smiled.

"I really didn't mean it to sound that way. I guess growing up with sisters has tainted my view on the whole getting dressed thing, eh?" He had a smile on his face. She shrugged and he continued. "It's alright, though. I'm in no hurry. You look nice, by the way. Blue suits you."

Adoo blushed at the compliment. She had never been happier for her coffee-toned skin than at that moment. She mumbled a thank you and bent her head to adjust her glasses in a bid to gather herself. *What's with me, for goodness' sakes? He says you look nice and you flush like some bumbling teen? Grow up, Ibi!*

She excused herself, trying to hide her embarrassment, and made a quick call to Mary, apologising for her lateness. Luckily, Mary had not been on time herself and agreed to meet her in a quarter of an hour.

"Honestly, Adoo, planning a wedding can be

excruciating," said Mary.

"And I hope you haven't moulded all the flowers for the cake because I need to change something small in the design. I hope it won't be a problem?"

After reassuring Mary, Adoo mumbled her thanks and hung up. They drove through the busy town centre bustling with traffic and people, trying to find a place to park on Ahmadu Bello Way.

"What about your car?" he asked after he'd managed to find a place.

"Oh, I'll go and get her as soon as I'm done with my meeting," she said. "Thanks again, Toby. I really appreciate it." He smiled and nodded. As she stepped out of the car he spoke again.

"Adoo, what's your phone number?"

She was confused. Why would he want her number? Most men avoided women with offspring, running as fast as possible in the opposite direction. Still surprised, she stammered out her number as he saved it into his phone.

"Maybe I'll call you sometime," he said, smiling, before driving off. She stared after him until the car rounded the corner and disappeared. Then she exhaled and turned to go into one of the restaurants that lined the city's main road, bemused at the turn of events. As much as she tried to dismiss it, she hoped Toby would keep to his word and call her. She would like that very much indeed.

# Four

Toby wasn't normally bothered by a heavy workload. In fact, he used work as a numbing agent and a way to pass his time. He considered himself very focused, which was why his recent preoccupation with Miss Adoo Ibi was surprising. It had been almost two weeks since he had dropped her off in town and he hadn't seen her since. But she kept popping up in his mind at the strangest times, like now.

Looking at the neatly organised stack of files that needed his urgent attention, he started to ask himself whether he didn't deserve a break after all. In two years he had single-handedly turned the club around and as a result Dare, the owner of the club, had begged him to stay on, enticing him with a higher salary, which he hadn't had the time to enjoy. *Man, you haven't been out and about in a while, have you?* Toby asked himself. *You need to relax a little ... and with some company for once.*

Toby knew without much effort who he would want to spend his leisure time with. He really couldn't understand why he was drawn to Adoo. The fact that she was a single mother wasn't exactly in her favour, at least not in the semi-conservative Nigerian setup.

"Eh? She get pikin?" He could almost hear some of his friends and family members admonishing him. *Why would a single young man like you want to involve yourself with a woman who has another man's child? And a son too?*

But he had never cared much about convention anyway and she seemed like someone out of the ordinary, a woman with hidden facets. There was no harm in calling her and asking her out, was there? He picked up his phone and called her. She answered on the second ring.

"Hello?" She sounded groggy, as though he had woken her from sleep.

He looked at the clock: 9.23pm. Did she really go to sleep that early? *Man, major mess up number one,* he chided himself.

"Oh … did I wake you? I'm sorry, I can call back …" he said, feeling like a schoolboy caught doing something wrong.

"No, no, Toby. It's fine. You *are* the Toby with the shiny Merc, aren't you?" He smiled at her offhand humour.

"Yes … yes it is. I'm still at the office."

"How sad," she chuckled.

"Sad … well, I don't … anyway how are you?" he said, tripping over his words. Very unlike him.

"I'm sleepy, Toby."

"Oh, OK … well I just wanted to call to see how you're doing and ask you if you'd like to join me for a drink at The Bar-Rage tomorrow evening around 9pm? I can pick you up if you'd like."

There was brief silence at the other end and Toby wondered if he had overstepped his bounds. He was almost ready to apologise, when she answered.

"That sounds like a plan. See you at my place at nine. No African time, please. I have a self-imposed curfew."

Toby felt pleased with himself as he hung up. He was actually looking forward to this date, sure that there would be more fascinating things to discover about Miss Adoo Ibi.

***

Adoo fidgeted in front of the mirror as she plucked an imaginary piece of lint from her light-blue T-shirt and smoothed her hands over her gypsy-style skirt, fashioned from different pieces of Ankara fabric. She had pulled her braids back into a ponytail and had put on a little more make-up than usual: smoky eyeshadow in addition to her usual kohl, with some shimmery nude lip gloss. She had not been out with a guy in a while and it didn't hurt to look a little more chic than usual.

Aduke had been only too glad to , clapping her hands in glee when Adoo came into her room the following morning to ask her, as she sat to loosen her braids.

"Zander is an angel," Aduke had said, "and his mother seriously needs to spend more time with an African Adonis!" Adoo laughed at her description.

"African Adonis? Hian! This one that you're introducing to mythology …"

"Eh, am I lying?" Aduke shrugged, lifting her hands back to her head.

Adoo put her hands on her hips. "Are you sure you shouldn't go with him instead, with the way you are excited for me? It's just a nice outing. Just a drink and small gist."

"Eh-hehn?" Aduke had exclaimed with a theatrical look of disbelief. "Look, my friend, you had better arrange yourself for this your 'drink and small gist'."

"No," Adoo had said, suddenly serious. "I don't want to look desperate because I'm not."

"This has nothing to do with being desperate. He called you and he asked you out, so the least you can do is appear presentable."

"Presentable? What do you mean by that?" Adoo had pouted in mock indignation. "What's wrong with the way I look?"

"Nothing is wrong with you." Aduke had raised her eyebrows as she scanned Adoo from head to toe. "You just need a little, erm … arranging, that's all."

Adoo chuckled to herself as she remembered the conversation. She hoped that she had "arranged" herself well enough. Not that she was doing it all for Toby's sake. Well, maybe she did choose the blue shirt because he had mentioned that blue suited her. Perhaps some part of her wanted to impress him?

A knock at the front door broke her reverie and she went to answer. It was Toby, his hands stuffed into the pockets of his slim-cut jeans. He looked relaxed and gorgeous in a light-grey cardigan with the sleeves pushed up to his elbows. She picked up the scent of an unfamiliar but pleasing perfume, something deep, woody and masculine. He raised his eyebrows in appreciation as he scanned her.

"Hello," he said. "I'm right on time, abi?" She nodded and he continued. "You look great, by the way, very … chic? Is that the right word to use?"

She nodded, smiling and feeling her face grow warm in response to his compliment. There was nothing lecherous about the way he looked at her. It was just … nice. The self-deprecating voice in her wanted to push the feelings of pleasure down.

*The only reason a man like this would look at you is to warm you up so he can eventually get what he wants and leave. Why would he be any different from Teremun? You know you're not one to turn heads.* Despite her best efforts, her inner defences had kicked in and a part of her shut down. She murmured a thank you and walked out, locking the door behind her.

Adoo sat quietly in the car, unsure how to start the conversation until Toby spoke first, to draw her out of her frozen state.

"So who's your son with? Zander, isn't it?"

"Oh, he's with Aduke."

"Zander. That's an unusual name. Not Nigerian, is it?" The mention of her son seemed to thaw her out a bit.

"Well, I decided Alexander was a little … heavy for him so I cut it shortened to Zander. I think it suits him perfectly. Besides, it's unique. How many Zanders do you know?"

"How old is he?"

"Three and acting every bit his age. Do you have any kids?"

"No. I have nieces and nephews though. Children are … challenging, to say the very least."

"And by 'challenging' do you mean a pain in the backside?" she asked, laughing. He responded by raising an eyebrow and shrugging.

Soon enough they were inside the compound of The Bar-Rage, where the parking lot was chock-full of cars of different sizes, colours and price tags. Adoo could see young men and women heading in two different directions. She noticed the older thirty-something 'yuppie' group moving towards a large glass door she figured was the entrance.

"Where are they going?" Adoo asked pointing towards a group of young ladies dressed in short, sparkly dresses accompanied by casually dressed young men who were heading towards a heavy wooden door shaded by French-style awning at the side of the building.

"To the nightclub, which is in the extension at the back. The front part of the building houses the lounge, karaoke bar and the food area where you met Emem," he said, giving her an amused look. She laughed at the memory.

"Ah yes, Emem. How is she, by the way?"

"Still nursing the wounds you inflicted," he said,

casting a sideways glance at her, a smile playing at the corners of his lips.

"Yes, well, I did let my temper get the best of me," she said quietly, feeling a little ashamed at the reminder.

"We all let certain things get the best of us sometimes, Adoo," he said. Adoo didn't have time to mull over what that statement might imply, as Toby was already pulling into the parking space reserved for him along the side of the building.

They both got out of the car at the same time and he walked around to her side as she stepped out. She noticed that he slowed a little, allowing her to walk ahead of him and set the pace. She thought it a sweet gesture.

She looked around, taking note of the well-kept lot. The grass was perfectly mown, looking soft and inviting, almost beckoning one to sit on it. The air bore a hint of eucalyptus and jasmine, with trees and shrubs bordering the compound walls.

"Wow ... it looks so well run," she said. "Well done."

"Thank you, we do our very best," he said, bowing his head with a flourish. "As you can see, there's a bit of a crowd tonight. I hope you're up to it?" he teased.

They walked into the lounge, which was built slightly below ground level – somewhat like a basement – so that they had to take a few steps down. It was furnished with soft leather couches in warm tones of orange, brick red and tan.

A few people sat on stools at the bar, sipping drinks and

chatting with the bartender. Easy R&B music played in the background. There was a steady hum of conversation mixed with a few shouts from those watching a football match on the large wall-mounted flatscreen TV on the far side of the room. Toby scanned the area, and waved at a few people he knew. They waved back and shouted greetings at him. He answered them all affably.

As they made their way towards the bar, Toby reached out for Adoo's hand, as though it was the most natural thing in the world to do. She hesitated, lightly clasping his fingers at first, before sliding her hand into his. He was struck by how perfectly her palm fitted into his. For an instant the din seemed to recede into the background as Toby's mind centred on the woman beside him. How long had it been since he had enjoyed the simple pleasure of holding a woman's hand? *Too long,* he thought. He introduced her to each person he spoke to and she in turn smiled and made small talk, ignoring the curiosity on some of their faces.

"Do you want something to drink?" he asked at the precise moment a goal was scored. The cheers were deafening and she looked at him and shook her head, indicating that she hadn't heard what he had said.

"Maybe we should go into the karaoke bar?" he asked when the noise died down. "It's a little rowdy out here."

"OK, that's cool."

"Let me go and order some drinks and snacks for us, first. What would you like?" She told him what she'd like and he went over to the bar, leaving her to her thoughts.

Adoo felt her palms sweating as Toby left to order their refreshments. She slowly rubbed her hands on her skirt, trying to shake off the strange mix of attraction and trepidation within her. Although she knew that he had only held her hand to keep her close, she'd had a brief longing. It wasn't as though she needed a man as such, but she had to admit there was a part of her that desired genuine companionship with someone of the opposite sex. This outing with Toby, as nice as it was turning out to be, could mean nothing but two friends spending time together. She had to get that into her mind. *We're friends*, she reminded herself, *and besides you don't trust men, especially the gorgeous ones, remember?*

Soon enough she saw him weaving his way back through the crowd and signalling to her. She joined him and they walked into the karaoke bar. It was less crowded than the main lounge. There were a few couches arranged around small tables, surrounding a small stage where the guy with the microphone was doing his best to croon along to Banky W's "Strong Thing". And, if his lack of coordination and slurred delivery was anything to go by, he might have had one strong drink too many.

People were scattered around the seating areas in groups, with their heads bent close, some in conversation and others studying the menu. The lighting here was more subdued, with soft hues of blue and low yellow casting muted shadows across the room.

Toby chuckled as the guy on stage hit a bad note, almost falling down in the process. One of his friends came to rescue him from further humiliation by taking the microphone from him.

"Na wa o. Can you see what people do for fun?" Toby said. "Sometimes when it's really loud, I can hear it in my office. Then I just put on my earphones." Adoo shook her head and smiled as they found an intimate corner to sit down. When they were seated, a pretty waitress came up to their table to serve their drinks: Coke for Adoo and tonic water for Toby. Adoo noticed the waitress casting furtive looks at Toby and when he caught her eye she appeared flustered, her hands shaking a little as she served. He thanked her and she flashed him a flirtatious smile, which from the slight smile he gave her, he either didn't catch or chose to ignore. She picked up the tray and left, leaving Adoo staring at her in amusement.

"Did you see the way she just looked at you?"

"Really? I didn't see anything unusual," he answered. He glanced roguishly at her, wiggling his eyebrows, and she bumped him playfully on the arm. He leaned back against the soft chaise longue and cocked his head to one side.

"So … what's your story, Adoo? Who are you and what are you doing in Jos?"

"I could ask you the same question, Toby."

He shook his head. "Nope, I asked you first, so no cheating. Go on, spill it."

Adoo shifted in her seat, feeling she had been put on the spot. True, she owed this man no explanations, but she didn't want to whitewash anything; her mistakes and her pain were her responsibility. Much of what had happened over the past four years had been as a result of her lapses in judgement. She had made mistakes, but who hadn't?

She cleared her throat before speaking. "I'm here in Jos because it's the perfect place to raise my son and have an easy-going life. I've had the opportunity to develop my cake-making and decorating skills by taking some short courses and tutorials and lots of practice. I love the fact that I'm able to do what I love and make a decent living."

"I've never actually got to know a cake maker," he said. "It sounds like something unusual. It must be interesting though."

"It is. It's also very cathartic," she answered. "Sure, Jos is not the most bustling city in Nigeria, but I'm fine with that: I like the pace."

"Why do I have the feeling that you just gave me the sanitised, factory-made version of your life?" he said gently.

"I don't know you well enough to give all the gory details," she said. He raised his brows and chuckled.

"Touché. Now it's my turn, I presume?"

Adoo nodded and he spoke. "There's nothing spectacular, I'm afraid. I have a brother and two sisters, and all but one live out of the country. My parents are in Kogi. No wife, no kids at the moment. No madness, leprosy or domestic abuse in my gene pool, as far as I know."

"And you've got a sense of humour too? My goodness, you are the stuff of every single-and-searching girl's dreams," Adoo quipped. She immediately regretted the comment. The last thing she wanted was to give him the impression that she was out to catch a man. He seemed to miss it completely though, his expression remaining unchanged. Adoo was relieved.

"And what are your dreams, Adoo, if you don't mind my asking?" He leaned forward slightly, pinning her down with his look. Her breath caught in her throat. She wasn't sure how to answer that. How long had it been since she had actually dared to dream about a life beyond what she had? There were the usual "if onlys", but actual dreams that could turn into life-changing events? She couldn't remember. She had spent so many years living life one day at a time that she hadn't actually sat down to think about the future.

"Sometimes life gets in the way of dreaming, Toby," she answered, looking down to avoid revealing too much of her inner turmoil.

"Not life, Adoo. People. People get in the way of dreams." She looked up and saw him regarding her with a frank stare; nothing untoward, but enough to unnerve her. He was too perceptive for her comfort. She decided to direct his comment back at him as a question.

"What would you know about that?"

"More than I would like," he answered, a faraway look coming over his face.

They were silent for a moment and then Bonnie Raitt's 'I Can't Make You Love Me' came on. No-one in the room paid attention to it except Adoo, whose ears had pricked up at the first strains of the song. The soft piano played a melancholy tune, echoes of anguish flowing through the melody.

She began to hum along.

"You know this song?" Toby asked. Know it? She had lived the song.

"There are few songs in this world that capture a moment of weakness as perfectly as this one."

He looked thoughtful for a moment before speaking. "You sing, don't you? Why don't you karaoke it then?" Adoo was just about to refuse when something in her pushed back. *Why not?* She got up slowly and went to the pick up the microphone. She brought it up to her mouth and began to sing the chorus.

# Five

Adoo's throaty, contralto voice, reminiscent of India Arie, flowed over the room. Toby had no idea she could sing so beautifully, capturing each note and making it hers. The noise in the room died down to silence as people turned to look and listen, held captived by Adoo's soulful crooning. She held the microphone with both hands and closed her eyes, completely bound by the song. She moved on to the second verse.

Toby sighed, wondering when he would ever escape the memories. Why did he have to remember such things on an easy-going night out? Why did they follow him everywhere?

It had been four years since the afternoon he had spent with Hannani. He had told her that he loved her that very day. She had not reciprocated the feeling. Their last conversation was seared into his memory:

"The best thing to do is to forget about it and move on," she had said. "And my future is with Bala." She moved her hand and her engagement ring glinted, casting a shard of light at him. A reminder that she would never be his.

"You are not an option, Toby," she had said. "You will always be my biggest mistake." And then she had walked away, not turning back, taking the pieces of his shattered heart with her.

\*\*\*

Adoo sang from her heart, letting the notes slide out of her, releasing some of her pain in the process. As the song drew to a close and she sang the last notes, she opened her eyes to find the entire room looking at her. She held her breath, unsure what to think. Then one by one they started to clap, most of them smiling and some shaking their heads in appreciation. As the applause mounted, she smiled, gave a slight bow and stepped off the platform.

She found Toby looking at her with an odd mixture of admiration and understanding as she approached. As she sat down, he leaned over and spoke.

"You're an amazing singer, Adoo. I had no idea you were so gifted."

"Thank you, Toby," she whispered.

"I don't think there is any more need for me to ask you what your story is." She looked at him in surprise, unsure what he meant. "You sang your story, Adoo. The way you sang the lyrics … it told me everything about you. That's your story, isn't it? 'I Can't Make you Love Me', is that it?" he asked.

Adoo had the sudden urge to burst into tears. She turned her face away, swallowing convulsively and willing herself not to cry. *Stop it,* she chided herself. *Don't make a complete idiot of yourself by crying in front of him. Stop being a sentimental fool and pull yourself together.*

"Um … thank you for the compliment," she finally managed. "I … well, I love singing. And that song is one of my favourites."

"You're avoiding my question, Adoo," Toby said, his eyes boring into hers. Adoo bristled, her defenses going up. *How dare he intrude in her life? What did he know of it?*

"I don't owe you any answers, Toby," she said abruptly. She immediately regretted her harshness.

Toby didn't skip a beat as he nodded, answering, "You're right, Adoo. I'm sorry … I didn't mean to pry." With that he leaned back, sipping his drink while Adoo cursed herself for ruining a lovely evening.

The drive back to her flat was fraught with tension. Neither of them knew what to say to each other.

Adoo felt miserable. Why did she have to do that? She had managed to place a wall between her and this appealing man with a few defensive words, but pride wouldn't let her admit it to him. Soon enough they were at her flat and she thanked him for the nice evening out.

Just as she was about to get out of the car his voice, low but firm, held her back. "You and I are really not that different, Adoo. It's easy to recognise someone with their defences up, if your own are exactly the same. Sometimes the walls we put up to protect ourselves end up being cages."

She turned to him, opening her mouth as though to say something, but then she closed her lips and pasted a fake smile on her face.

"That's a thought to chew on for a while," she said too breezily and she got out of the car. She gave him a small wave, pushed open the gate and slipped into the compound.

***

Adoo didn't hear from Toby for a week and that bothered her. She figured she had pushed him away for good. He had tried to get her to open up and she had reacted with hostility. Nobody would want that kind of treatment. By the end of the week, when Adoo couldn't stand the suspense any longer, she swallowed her pride and dialled his number late one evening.

"Adoo." He spoke her name as though he was making a statement of great importance.

Hearing his voice brought a surge of delight to her, as though everything was as it should be. How could a man she hardly knew arouse such confusing feelings in her? She had rehearsed what she would say to him but when she opened her mouth an entirely different thing came out.

"I'm not usually such an emotional basket case," she blurted. *Oh really? Well you sound just like one right now,* she thought, kicking herself. *Don't be surprised if he warns you to stay away and hangs up immediately.*

Toby laughed. "OK, Adoo. That's good to know. I'm glad we got that out of the way."

His response put her at ease. "Look, I'm sorry if I seemed a bit cold or standoffish the other night. It wasn't my intention. It's just that … well, you hit a nerve and I had a kneejerk reaction."

"I thought as much," he said. "And I really do understand where you're coming from, Adoo. Maybe I shouldn't have pushed it too much myself. You actually don't know me well enough to give me all the details of your inner life."

They said nothing for a few moments and Adoo scrambled around in her head for something to say to fill the awkward silence.

Toby filled the gap instead. "There's something about you that I recognise in myself. And if you ever need to … talk, just give me a call. No strings attached."

Adoo's eyebrows rose in surprise and a slow smile spread across her face. "Oh really? Well, I just might take you up on that offer, Toby. No strings attached, abi?"

"Anytime," he said. "And now, if you don't mind, I have to go. I'd like to get home and try and catch some sleep or else I might become a vampire." She chuckled as they said their goodbyes and hung up.

She thought about their conversation. He had just made it clear that he viewed her as a friend. She knew she should be relieved at that; it placed them on a purely platonic level and that was where she'd preferred to be with men since Teremun. *No strings attached – right?* Then why did she feel such a dull disappointment? What was she to do with her attraction to him? She sighed and tried to get to sleep.

***

Two weeks later, Adoo's phone rang late in the evening.

"Hey, I'll be heading home in a few minutes. Would you like some pizza?" Toby asked. "I can bring it over. We haven't seen each other in a while and I just thought I'd see how you were doing." Adoo was taken aback at how pleased she was at the prospect of seeing him again.

"That sounds good," Adoo said, trying not to sound too enthusiastic. *A girl has to have a little bit of pride.*

"I'll be over in 20 minutes or so," he said.

"See you then."

As they hung up Adoo mused over their growing friendship. They had spoken a few times since she had called him that night. She couldn't recall ever being so at ease with a man. He was a good listener and had a way of steering conversation in comfortable directions. He laughed at her wry sense of humour and her ability to laugh even at herself. She was learning a lot about management from him, as he gave her suggestions on how to make the most of her business. They had argued hotly about the 2015 elections, which had ended in Toby admitting her superior debating skills. She laughed at his vehemence when discussing the use of nuts in cooking, something he had an avid dislike for.

However, they skirted more personal issues like heartbreak and relationships. It was as though both of them were waiting for the other to open up first. Not being one to hide things for too long, she wanted to tell Toby about Teremun as soon as it was appropriate. Better

47

to get her baggage out of the way so they could move forward. Perhaps once she did he would open up to her too?

She threw on a T-shirt and a faded pair of jeans and checked to make sure Zander was still fast asleep on the bed. Aduke was watching TV in the living room and looked up in surprise when she saw Adoo coming out of her bedroom wearing a light cardigan to ward off the chill.

"Toby is coming over with some pizza," Adoo explained. "I'm going outside to meet him." Aduke looked like she wanted to say something but then appeared to think better of it, nodding instead. She turned back towards the TV as Adoo walked out of the flat and towards the gate of the estate. The phone rang and Toby told her that he was approaching the estate.

The mai-guard opened the side gate for her and she slowly walked out. True to his word, she saw the bright headlights of his car round the corner. They blinded her for an instant before the car rumbled to a stop next to the gate.

He stepped out of the vehicle, his tall frame silhouetted against the navy hues of the night. The full moon offered just enough light for her to make out his form but not enough to catch his facial expressions.

"Hello," she said, suddenly feeling tongue-tied. He walked towards her, hands in pockets.

"Hello, Adoo," he said, his voice rolling over her and

warming her from within. "I left the pizza in the car. You can take it when you're ready to go in, abi?"

"Thanks, Toby," she said. "It's really nice of you to go out of your way for me."

"Ba damuwa. After all, what are friends for? Everybody needs someone to stretch a little on their behalf every now and then. Besides, you're one of the nicest people I've met in Jos, you know."

"Nice, eh? That is one of the blandest adjectives in the English language."

Toby laughed. "Oh, and now you're a grammarian? OK then how about, you're the coolest cake-maker female friend I have in Jos? Better adjectives?"

Adoo smiled, nodding. "Eh hehn, that's better."

Toby smiled back and they let the pleasantness of the moment tide them over in silence. Adoo looked down, shaking her head. "You know … I haven't exactly had many male friends since Teremun."

"I take it Teremun is 'the guy'? The one who changed things for you?"

"Changed things would be putting it politely," she replied.

"It seems we all have someone like that … someone who hurt us so badly we almost shut down."

"Teremun is Zander's father."

"Adoo, you don't have to …"

"I want to, Toby," she said, looking up at him. He nodded.

"Do you want to sit down? Maybe we should go to the car." They walked in companionable silence and sat in the car. They left the doors open so a cool breeze could pass through. She began to speak haltingly, unsure of how much to reveal, yet feeling compelled to open up. That was the effect this man had on her and it was as exhilarating as it was disturbing.

"I've always thought that I'm average, in looks as well as in life. It really never bothered me much. I just took it as my lot and I was never bitter about it," she said. "I'm the classic middle child, landing right smack between three sisters and a brother. Our family is comfortably off so I never wanted for anything when I was growing up."

He put his hands behind his head, stretching to be more comfortable, his eyes never leaving her face. His movement sent out a warm wave of perfume from him, the same scent she remembered, a very refined signature. Adoo kept talking, refusing to be distracted by his appeal.

"So when Teremun, who happened to be gorgeous, witty and with prospects, started toasting me, I was so flattered I ignored all the warning signs. It never occurred to me that the only reason he wanted me was because none of my sisters would give him the time of day. He just wanted to use me to get to my family's money. And I wasn't smart enough to get that."

"You couldn't have known that, Adoo. He manipulated you and he's the one to blame for that, not you."

"That's the thing, Toby, I let him. My family, especially

my father, hated Teremun and that only made me hang on tighter to him. I guess it was some form of rebellion against Dad. Mama was too timid to tell me that I was making a mistake. I packed out of my parents' home and moved in with him, in his face-me-I-face-you room. I thought I was in heaven and that 'love' would see us through. Then I got pregnant."

Toby shook his head. "And did he take responsibility for that?" Adoo made a dismissive sound in her throat.

"Once he realised that he had no chance of getting anything from my family, he wasted no time leaving me. I came back from the market one day and found that he had changed the padlock to the room and locked me out. I waited on the steps until it got dark. I tried calling him but his phone was switched off. It was 10pm when it finally dawned on me that he wasn't coming back and that he had left me."

Toby's forehead creased as a look of anger crossed his face. "Did you have the baby there?" .

"No, I moved to Jos to stay with Aduke just before Zander was born. And the rest, as they say, is history," Adoo said.

"Making that move must have been hard for you," he said. Adoo smiled and shrugged.

"It wasn't easy, but it was the best thing to do. I've got Zander, a good business and business partner, supportive friends and a great church family. Everything I need, I have," she said. He nodded, running his hand over his head.

"And your family? Do you communicate much – if you don't mind my asking?"

"We talk every now and then," she said. She and her parents had a tense relationship and she didn't really know how to explain that.

"Then I guess Zander is your main family now, abi?" Toby said, a smile playing at his lips.

"Zander is my joy, my sunshine. He is living proof that God has given me a second chance." Adoo felt tears spring to her eyes and realised too late that one had already snaked down her cheek. She made no move to wipe it away. "I am still in awe of the fact that someone so beautiful could have come out of such a dark time in my life. Zander deserves stability and I have to be very careful who I expose him to. I owe it to him."

"And you? What do you owe yourself, Adoo?"

"Me? Well … I guess I haven't thought much about that. It's been me, Zander and Jesus, I guess. I think that's all the male company I can handle for now," she said, smiling through her tears. Toby reached out and wiped her tears with his right thumb, his fingers resting next to her ear. She closed her eyes and, when she opened them, his expression was open.

"Look, Toby, I'm not out to give you a sob story. I'm not into handouts of any kind. It's just a painful part of my life that has made me who I am now."

Toby didn't answer. He put his hands on either side of her face, and, before she had time to analyse his actions, he leaned towards her. She almost protested, but then the stronger part of her let go.

Their lips met in the softest, sweetest kiss she had ever experienced. When they pulled apart, she didn't know what to say as her heart hammered in her chest. He finally cleared his throat.

"I'd normally fill this awkward silence with a witty comment. But … I seem to be at a loss for words," he said. Adoo, feeling the same, nodded.

He continued, "I have to confess … I've wanted to do that since the day I saw you changing that tyre." Adoo raised her brows and laughed.

"Really? When I was covered in oil and cursing my car? That is … unusual." Toby shrugged and they both smiled.

"I hope you don't mind, though … the kiss, I mean. I don't mean to come on too strong," he said, sounding unsure of himself. Adoo found his awkwardness very endearing.

"No. No, I don't mind it at all, Toby," she said, in a bid to put him at ease. She was finding it hard to think clearly and was suddenly overwhelmed with shyness. She needed to get back to the flat, back to her son and her senses.

"Toby, I've really enjoyed our chat, but I have to go now," she said softly.

He nodded, saying, "I'll walk you to the gate."

She smiled and stepped out of the car, standing up

just as he reached her side. "So when do I get to meet Zander?" he asked, as they walked slowly towards the gate. Her eyes locked onto his and, despite the fact that the only light illuminating the area was moonlight, Adoo could tell that his motives were innocent. He genuinely wanted to meet Zander.

"How does this weekend sound?"

"That sounds good. If he's anything like you I'm sure he'll be … entertaining."

She laughed and he handed her the box with the now cold pizza just as they reached the gate. He leaned over and brushed her cheek with a kiss. A part of her was disappointed and another relieved. It wasn't that she didn't want him to. She just preferred to give the impression of 'keeping it together' and not let him know just how close she had come to being completely swept away and confused by a single kiss. She was finding it hard to struggle with her juvenile butterflies-in-the-tummy feelings whenever she was around him.

As she approached her flat she thought about the evening, especially the kiss – the crowning moment. She was a little shocked about it and even more perturbed that she had not felt the need to resist at all. She had never been liberal with her kisses and yet this man had made her feel giddy with that kiss. Disturbing, she thought. She opened the door and walked into her flat, aware then that she had a small smile on her face.

# Six

Toby had not planned to kiss her, a dangerous move on his part. He could not understand the effect Adoo was having on him.

He had always liked the conventional, high-fashion beauties, but he was also very keen on intelligence – something Adoo obviously possessed in spadefuls. The fact that she had strong opinions and wasn't a pushover made her personality even more compelling. Despite his mental criteria for his 'type' of woman, he found that Adoo didn't easily fit any mould, at least not in theory. She seemed sensitive, with her eyes reflecting deep pools of emotion, but there was an undercurrent of resilience and strength that could be both an advantage and a barrier to anyone seeking to come into her life. The only other time he had strayed from his 'type' as far as women were concerned had brought him a whole lot of trouble.

What made him even more uncomfortable about the whole issue was the fact that he didn't feel entirely in control of the direction things were going. He had promised himself that he would never give a woman power over him, the way he had done with Hannani. He had learned that any woman who got his heart in her hands had the potential to crush it and he was loath to give anyone that chance again.

He had to admit that Adoo stirred him physically. But

there was too much potential drama in her life and the sensible part of him did not to want to get entangled. And yet entangled he was, by his own hand.

*My guy, you've been without a woman for too long. All this is just an itch you need to scratch,* he reasoned. *Step back to the 'just friends' category with her, hang out with her and her son, and everything will be fine. No strings attached. Just friends.*

It all sounded fine and logical in his head. But Toby had seen 'logic' come crashing down before.

***

Toby felt totally relaxed and at peace with himself as he, Adoo and Zander walked together through Jos Wildlife Park. It was a lovely day, with clear blue skies and the smell of earth and greenery around. Families milled about and snack vendors were having a field day with customers. Someone had set up a music system and the sound of Nigerian pop songs floated through the air. He couldn't remember the last time he felt so at ease with another person, let alone a child. Warning bells began to ring in his head, telling him to slow down and take a few steps back from this woman and her son and not allow them to become too important to him. He willed the internal alarms away, determined not to let anything spoil his leisure.

"When I was a boy like you I wanted to live in the jungle, like Mowgli in *The Jungle Book*," Toby said.

Zander looked up at him, a little puzzled.

"Uncle, what is 'junga boo'?" he asked, scrunching up his nose, so like Adoo's.

He looked at Adoo in surprise and she shrugged. "Er … wait, he hasn't watched *The Jungle Book*?" She shook her head slowly. "Kai, how can the child of any self-respecting person raised in the 1980s not watch *The Jungle Book*? In fact, I will go to those CD guys at Railway, and I'll look for it," he said. "Maybe you can bring him over to watch it?"

"Bring him over to your house?" Adoo asked in surprise.

Toby rolled on, not really thinking. "Why not? I've got a really large flatscreen TV with a mega sound system and I'm sure he'd love it," he said. He realised that he was inviting potential trouble over to his turf. But it was too late to back down. He sighed at his carelessness and went on.

"Er … that is if you don't mind. I wouldn't want to take it for granted that you'd like to come over …" he said, leaving the sentence unfinished.

She smiled and answered, "No, no I don't mind. You're so right. He should watch it. Besides this, your big TV and sound thing sounds like something he would like anyway."

Equal amounts of pleasure and foreboding coursed through Toby as she agreed. He tried to appear as casual about it as possible, speaking in an exaggerated whisper.

"I'm a closet cartoon fan myself, but don't tell anyone; it would ruin my PR in this town. Besides, you look like someone who watches the Disney Channel in secret."

"I will not admit to anything, Oga," she said. "And thank you for giving me something to blackmail you with later." They laughed, following Zander who had run off to look at the elephants.

*** 

When Toby came around to pick them up after Sunday service, Zander had reached a fever pitch of excitement and it was all Adoo could do to keep him from jumping around in Toby's car. She stole glances at him to gauge if he was running out of patience with Zander's antics but he seemed to be taking everything in his stride, calmly distracting Zander before he got truly disruptive.

His house was much bigger than she had anticipated and before she could stop herself she asked, "And you live in this huge place all alone?" She bit her tongue at her forwardness. *What, do you want him to think you're hinting at moving in with him or something?*

Luckily for her, he didn't seem to pick up on her gaffe, answering in a matter-of-fact tone, "Yes it is quite big ... but then I've got all the amenities like light, water and security so it's worth having a few extra rooms."

As they walked in he asked them to make themselves at home while he went upstairs to change. Adoo took advantage of his absence to have a look around. The house was neat; that much impressed her. The furniture and décor was quite simple, with everything in smooth lines and neutral blacks and greys. The furniture looked like it was straight out of a catalogue, all with Scandinavian-esque bent pine, but she could tell that it had been locally made by a skilled carpenter probably from Delta State. He had blinds rather than curtains in the windows and the rugs on the tiled living room and dining floor had geometric patterns in black and grey. The dining table and coffee table had smooth polished surfaces, with no tablecloths or decorations. There were a few artsy photographs of 1950s African-American jazz singers on the stark white walls. Displayed on a red-brick mantlepiece with a faux fireplace were some photographs of people who she assumed were his family. The main splash of colour came from a vine that grew in a planter that served as a divider between the living room and dining areas.

He had a large home entertainment system at the far side of the expansive living room with tiny speakers placed unobtrusively in the corners. Zander gazed at the whole array with eyes wide in amazement and gripped her hand tightly. Toby soon came back downstairs, dressed in a pair of jeans and a white T-shirt that showed off his physique. He looked gorgeous. Adoo couldn't tell if he was aware of the effect he had on her.

"I wasn't sure if you had lunch after the service so I got some fried rice and chicken before picking you up. I hope you approve?"

Adoo didn't have a chance to say a word as Zander's ears pricked up at the mention of chicken. He shrieked with joy and leaped up, pulling his hand out of her grasp and running to Toby, bumping into his knees and nearly knocking him over. Toby laughed in surprise as Zander repeated "Chinkin, chinkin, chinkin!" like a nursery rhyme.

"Wow … if that's his reaction to chicken then what will he do if I tell him I got i-c-e-c-r-e-a-m for dessert?" he said, looking up at Adoo, mirth in his eyes. She couldn't recall the last time Zander had been so happy around male company and she didn't want to confuse her gratitude to Toby for something more.

They sat down to eat in front of the TV, sitting on the floor while they watched the cartoon with lunch on the floor. Zander yelled in delight at the antics in the movie and attempted to sing some of the songs, albeit off-key. Adoo's mind wandered as the three of them sat in Toby's living room.

*This feels so right. I feel like we belong here, as if I've come home. I can't remember being this content and comfortable around a man. And Zander likes him.*

Toby and Zander laughed together as the little boy asked questions and Toby answered patiently. She couldn't hear the exact words but the tone was all she needed to hear to understand the message.

*He should be running as fast as he can in the opposite direction, away from me … but he's coming closer and,*

*Lord help me, I don't want to stop him. Let me not make a mistake and give my heart away too quickly. Let this not be Teremun Part Two.*

\*\*\*

Hours later, after a marathon bout of watching cartoons, Zander lay sprawled out on the thick living room rug, fast asleep, and Toby and Adoo stood in the kitchen sipping mugs of tea in companionable silence. It was dark outside and the hum of the generator obliterated any sounds made by nature. The navy sky lit up sporadically with distant lightning: a sure warning of rain to come. The security lights cast a fluorescent blaze over the estate as flying insects flitted about the kitchen window. Toby had put one of his CDs into the player when Zander had fallen asleep and the soulful voice of Ryan Tedder as he sang to Far East Movement's 'Rocketeer' filtered into the kitchen. Adoo nodded her head to the rhythm and hummed along. Toby smiled, pleased that they had similar taste in music.

His mind began to wander and Adoo's voice brought his thoughts back home.

"You don't sleep very well, do you?" She pushed her braids away her face with one hand as she spoke.

"Why do you say that?"

She shrugged lightly. "You always look a little tired, like you've got a tremendous weight on your shoulders. Your working hours must interfere with your sleep, too."

He smiled and nodded. "You're right, I don't sleep that well. I don't know why. And it's not really my working hours because I can shift them around. I don't want to use pills because they can be addictive."

"Maybe you have too much on your mind, Toby."

"Any suggestions?" He looked at her and he could have sworn she began to blink a little faster, but she seemed to regain her composure a moment later.

"Maybe you need to unload a bit?" she asked, raising her eyebrows at him. He shrugged lightly, trying to remain casual and she went on.

"Toby, it's a bit unfair, I think, that you know almost all there is to know about me and I know very little about you," she said, looking at him pointedly.

Toby had known that, with more time spent together, the moment would come when he would have to lay his soul bare and allow Adoo to see the scars he had received. The wounds were no more stinging than hers, though, he had to admit. He hesitated, knowing that revelation usually meant vulnerability, and he wasn't too sure he wanted to appear vulnerable.

"Everyone has that moment in life when pain has a name. Yours was Teremun. Mine was Hannani," he said, his voice even as he looked out the window.

"Hannani." Adoo whispered her name, almost in awe. "Wow, what a beautiful name. And was she? Beautiful, I mean?"

Toby leaned back against the kitchen counter, and tried to conjure up Hannani's image in his mind.

"Not conventionally, I guess. But she had … something. She had a spark in her, a kind of vitality that I had never seen in any other woman. She was full of laughter, but she could speak her mind, regardless of what others thought. She could be as sweet as honey or bite like a viper."

"You make her sound so poetic," Adoo said, her eyes soft. Toby let out a choked laugh that exuded cynicism.

"Oh, I thought she was. We had been friends for years and she even started to date one of my closest friends. I can't really pinpoint the time I started to fall for her."

"Friends fall for each other all the time, Toby," she said gently. He shook his head and took a sip of tea and looked out of the window again. The view was the same as it had always been, shrubs and the side view of his neighbour's house, nothing out of the ordinary. But, today, he found himself studying a crack he had never paid attention to and he noticed a few blooms on the shrubs. *How odd*, he thought. He spoke even as he looked.

"I tried to hide how I felt about her. I didn't think it would do any good. Then one day she came to my flat in tears, telling me she had heard that her boyfriend had cheated on her. I knew he had … issues, but I had always kept quiet about them. I held her close as she cried, tried to comfort her and ..." He looked at Adoo and shrugged.

Adoo bit her lip and set her now-tepid tea down on the counter. "You went too far, didn't you?" she asked. He gave an almost imperceptible nod. He was not surprised at her perception, and was grateful for the fact that she seemed so in tune with him at that moment.

"She wouldn't talk to me afterwards and she avoided me. But by that time I was so in love with her I didn't really care about pride."

"Pride is usually the first thing to go, isn't it?" Adoo said, almost to herself.

"Soon after that, she and my friend announced that they were engaged."

"I'm sorry, Toby," she said.

"What for? You didn't do anything," he answered. She took a step towards him.

"No, but I know what it means to feel that deeply for someone and not have the feeling returned. And I am sorry you had to go through that."

"Everyone has to go through at least one moment of hurt."

"That doesn't make it easier, though."

"But it makes you stronger. And I'd like to think I'm stronger now. A better man, I hope."

"You're definitely better, Toby. I think you're great," she said, her eyes clear and unguarded. Toby saw something reflected in them that he didn't feel ready to deal with. But he found himself drawn in.

He felt a surge of affection for her. "You really should be more careful about your tendency to see the best in people. You let your guard down. This might just be a sob story I'm feeding you … 419, you know."

"It isn't a sob story and why should I have my guard up with you? Are you out to hurt me?"

She reached out to touch his arm and he grasped her hand and pulled her close into an embrace. She felt so right in his arms, her warmth spreading over him as she held him. They stood there for some seconds until he tipped her chin up and looked at her. Her eyes gave him all the indication he needed and he slowly lowered his head.

Their lips met in a kiss that set him on fire. She clung on to him, returning the kiss with fervour. He almost lost all sense of restraint as he held her and he could have sworn he saw fireworks behind his closed lids. His hands began to wander and Adoo made no move to stop him. Images began to whirl around in his head of him and Adoo and he tried to think of the best way to get her upstairs to …

"Mummy?"

That one word, said with a mixture of curiosity and panic, coming from the living room made Adoo open her eyes in shock and push Toby away abruptly. She put her hands to her cheeks, looking mortified.

He regained his balance, feeling disappointed that their kiss had come to such an abrupt end.

"Er … I think I should go and check on him," she said, hurrying away and leaving Toby in a dishevelled state in the kitchen.

Toby exhaled slowly and ran his hand over his head, wondering what had come over him. He wanted Adoo. Period. There was nothing clean-cut or honourable about it. If it had not been for Zander he was quite sure he would have tried to get her into his bed. And he wasn't sure he felt bad about that. *We are both adults and can do as we want without the whole messy business of 'love' coming into it, right?*

He heard music coming from the other room, the theme song for the beginning of another cartoon. *Good, she has figured out how to occupy Zander.* A minute or two later she came back in, looking a little more composed. It was clear from the look in her eyes he was probably not 'getting lucky'.

"Er ... I think I need to get going. Tomorrow is Monday and I have to prepare for the week," she said.

"There's more than enough space for you and Zander here. Why don't you just take a load off and relax? You don't have to go today," he said, without thinking. Immediately he realised that had been a mistake, especially judging from Adoo's expression, which hardened and became shuttered.

Toby could have kicked himself for his blunder. *You've gone and messed up, guy,* Toby thought, cursing himself. He had come across as a lecher and that hadn't been his intention at all.

"Adoo ... I don't mean it like that. I just ..." he stumbled.

'It's fine, Toby. Can you take us home?" she said, her tone even.

He thought about saying more and explaining himself but in the end he thought it prudent to keep silent and take her home. They probably both needed to clear their heads anyway.

"Alright then, let's go," he said. She nodded and went to the living room to get Zander.

\*\*\*

Adoo battled to sleep that night, tossing in her bed, until she gave up on sleep and got up. She went to the dining table, where her fondant moulding paraphernalia was scattered about and fondant flowers and leaves were drying. She mixed some icing colour, picked up her paintbrush and began to paint details onto the flowers, passing time.

About an hour later, she went to the kitchen to make a cup of Ovaltine. *Maybe that will help me sleep.*

As she sat on the couch sipping the hot malt drink, she thought about the events of that evening. A hot flush came to her face as she recalled the kiss she and Toby had shared at his house. They had crossed a line and stepped from the no-man's-land of platonic friendship into something different. She heard a creak and looked up to see Aduke walking out of her bedroom, rubbing her eyes, her hair tucked into her sleeping hairnet.

"What is this?" Aduke asked groggily. "Only witches come out at this time to conduct their business." Adoo chuckled and motioned for her to sit down next to her. Aduke plopped down, looking at Adoo with sleep-blurred eyes.

"Don't you know you and I are connected in spirit, so, when you don't sleep, I don't sleep either?" Adoo smiled and shook her head.

"Kai Aduke, don't mind me. I'm just confused over this Toby issue."

"Why?"

"Things are … well, changing. He kissed me. Really well."

Aduke raised her eyebrows. "Wow. Kissed, ehn? I'm guessing it wasn't the 'greet one another with a Holy kiss' kind, abi?" Adoo shook her head. Aduke harrumphed and continued. "So, did you kiss him back?" Adoo felt the warmth creep into her face again and silently thanked God for her complexion.

"Yes, I kissed him back – well sef. In fact, if Zander hadn't called out to me, I don't know what would have happened."

"I think you know very well what would have happened, Adoo. And are you ready for that?" Aduke asked, dead serious now, all traces of fatigue and jest gone.

"No, I'm not. He opened up to me, which is a big deal for me. But I don't want to become anyone's sexual therapy, no matter how charming or fine the man is."

"Not every man is Teremun, Adoo," Aduke said. "It's not fair to assume that's all Toby wants from you."

"He suggested that Zander and I stay overnight. I don't think he really thought it through or meant anything bad but …"

Aduke whistled through her teeth. "Wow. Not a good idea if you don't want 'things' to happen."

They were silent for a moment, each with her thoughts. Then Aduke spoke, her voice low and her look frank.

"You're falling for him, aren't you?"

Adoo closed her eyes, exhaling slowly. "I don't want to."

"It sounds like you can't really help it."

"It's too soon. I don't know him well enough."

"Then get to know him more."

Adoo didn't have a suitable response so she kept quiet. Aduke was right. The best way for her to really make a proper decision was to get to know Toby more. And she had to admit that it was something she was very happy to do.

# Seven

Thoughts of Adoo came into Toby's head at the most inopportune times. He was trying his best to listen to Dare, the owner of The Bar-Rage, but was finding it difficult to do so. He remembered her bright eyes after he had kissed her the first time. Then his mind went to the kiss they'd shared in his kitchen: electrifying. Toby couldn't help the slow, smug smile that came to his lips at the memory. Then, just as quickly as the smile appeared, it faded as he remembered his clumsy blunder at his house: asking her to stay over. He wondered how he would be able to manoeuvre his way back into her good books.

He came back to the present, noticing that there was silence in the office. He saw Dare looking at him with indignation.

"Eh? I'm telling you about how armed robbers stole 30K from me and you're smiling? With guns, fa! Haba guy, na so e be?" Dare's pained expression only made Toby want to smile more but he checked himself, forcing a sober expression on his face.

"Oh, sorry, man. Something just crossed my mind."

"Eh hehn ... before I forget, remember the case I told you about? You know, the architect guy that claims that I didn't pay him for the building plans in Kaduna? Well, he wants to take the company to court ..."

Toby nodded. Dare continued, "I need us to win the

case o! We need the best lawyer …" Dare's eyes took on a faraway look that Toby recognised; one he got when he was about to go on a new tangent. He decided to take on the conversation from there to ensure that Dare wouldn't go on. He really was too distracted to continue with anything too serious.

"Don't worry about getting a lawyer. I know the perfect one for this type of case: James Okeke. We were in school together. I'll get in touch with him," Toby said, and then changed the subject. "See … there's this new apprentice cook we are trying out and he makes really good shawarma. Maybe you should try it and tell me what you think?" Dare's rotund frame spoke volumes and Toby knew exactly what would work with him.

Dare's eyes lit up, his love for food overshadowing his taste for conversation and Toby picked up the phone and called the kitchen. Then he slowly got up.

"Er … Dare, there's a very important call I need to make now so please excuse me. I'll be back later in the evening. We go see, abi?"

As soon as he got into his office he called Adoo, readying his mind for a possible frosty reception.

"Eh-hehn, well done, Mr Manager," Adoo said, a mock whine in her voice. "You just decided to *post* me for over a week: no calls, not even a 'Hi, how are you' to show you care if I'm still alive, abi?" He was unprepared for the sense of relief that swept over him at hearing her voice.

"Haba, it's not like that. I've been busy," he said.

"Haven't we all? I'm not happy with you anyway."

"OK, what can I do to make it up to you?"

"Come and see me … in church. I've got choir practice and I finish up in about forty minutes. Can you do that?" Her voice was soft and melodious, like soothing balm. Toby was ready to drop everything and go to see her, all pride thrown to the wind. *OK, this is interesting … you're ready to act on impulse minus any sense of male ego. Always a bad idea*, he chided himself.

"Give me the directions and I'll be there," he said. "But you owe me a gallon of petrol for all these runs I'm doing."

Half an hour later he pulled into the driveway of Adoo's church. The church was in a compound surrounded by a low fence, on the low hills between Tudun Wada area and Rantya, near Adoo's flat. It was a nondescript compressed brick building, whitewashed with emulsion paint.

He parked the car in the lot and climbed out. As he entered the church he was pleasantly surprised, wondering at how the interior so belied the plain exterior. The foyer was tiled and polished, and from where he stood he could see that the auditorium was covered in carpet. The doors were flanked by potted palms reflected in windows that had been polished to perfection. The ceiling was high and the fans suspended from it circulated cool around the room.

He recognised Adoo's voice immediately he stepped

72

into the auditorium, the carpet muffling his steps so that he was barely noticed. The choir was on the podium and the choirmaster gesticulated as music poured from speakers mounted on the walls.

A few people were milling about and he nodded in greeting to those who noticed him. He found a seat in the back row closest to the entrance, scanning the stage for Adoo, and finding her immediately. His eyes rested on her as she sang. Her attention seemed to be focused on the choirmaster. Once again he was carried away by her voice as he listened to her sing an old hymn. How she managed to take a song so antiquated and bring it to life in the minds and ears of her listeners, he had no idea.

He didn't know how long he sat there transfixed, but at the end of her solo the choirmaster called them together to say a thing or two. She looked up suddenly, her eyes meeting his and she smiled, winking mischievously. *So she was aware of my presence all along, was she?*

He smiled and nodded, waiting. Soon enough, after she had spoken to one or two people, she broke away from the group and walked towards him, her face creased in a smile.

"I saw you when you were looking for a seat. So … you're here."

"Yes, I'm here: thank you for stating the obvious," he joked. She laughed.

"Making fun of me in church, eh? I'll deal with you."

"Then I'll just grab you and kiss you in front of all

your brethren. That should give everyone enough gist to last for a week." Toby could have kicked himself for making mention of kisses or any form of bodily contact with her, especially since their last meeting had ended so awkwardly.

Adoo's eyes widened and she appeared flustered, muttering under her breath. He felt the urge to pull her into his arms for a hug but restrained himself: no need to make a spectacle of them both.

Besides, he noticed more than a few curious glances in their direction and he didn't want to make her fodder for gossip or unwelcome questions. He decided to change the subject.

"Where's Mr Zander? I didn't see him when I came in," he said, looking around him.

"Oh, he's in the media section with the guys handling all the microphones, sound systems and such. He should be out any moment." As if on cue there was a shriek from the back of the church and they saw Zander racing towards them, a broad smile on his face, his arms spread wide. He ran towards Toby who picked him up and swung him around.

"Uncle Toby! Uncle Toby!" he shouted. Toby held Zander in his arms, listening with a look of rapt interest as Zander tried to narrate, in jumbled sentences, his experiences in the media booth. As Zander spoke Toby stole a side glance at Adoo and winked.

They walked out together, Toby listening to Zander as

he babbled on and Adoo saying her goodbyes to the choir members as they passed by.

"I'm glad you're here," she said, a warm smile lighting up her features. For that moment it seemed as though they were the only ones in the compound and Toby felt a familiar yet unwelcome stirring somewhere deep within him, a place he preferred to keep locked up. *No way, man, not this.* He decided to break the unspoken communication by changing the subject.

"I liked the hymn you sang, by the way. Brought back memories of my childhood, going to church with my parents."

"Then maybe you should start going to church again. You'd be surprised at what you'll rediscover." He shrugged noncommittally.

There was silence for a moment before she spoke.

"Look … about that day at your house and the kiss … and then you suggesting I stay over," she began and then stopped, leaving the phrase hanging in the air. Toby took a deep breath, and then plunged in.

"I don't regret that kiss at all, Adoo. I wanted to do it and your response showed me you wanted the same thing. I regret my careless words, though. I really didn't mean to make it seem like I just wanted you to shack up with me overnight."

"Shack up with you, like kwanan gida? So, it would be that easy, eh?" Her voice was quiet, but he picked up the change in tone. She narrowed her eyes and he attempted to calm the rising fire he was sure was forming.

"I do not think you are easy or …"

"You think I'd just jump into bed with you? Just like that?" This time the annoyance in her voice was fully evident.

Toby made a frustrated sound in his throat before he spoke. "Now you're being unreasonable, Adoo. Look, you and I are not kids. It was a great moment and I'm thinking this could progress to something more. I like you a lot and it's obvious we're attracted to each other. What's wrong with that?"

"I just don't want you thinking that I … well, I can't … the sex thing …" she faltered.

"Sex thing?" he asked, his expression one of genuine confusion. "Eh-hehn … continue. I'm listening." He leaned sideways against his car, his eyes squarely on Adoo's face.

"Toby, I made up my mind to wait until the right time. I'm not ready for all the wahala all this sex stuff brings. Been there, done that. Besides, I pushed my luck with God and He still let me have Zander. I'm not going to play with Him on this issue. Besides, I'm really big on respect …"

The resolution in her voice showed that she wouldn't budge and would walk away if she had to, something Toby battled out within himself. *Let her go, let her walk away, man. It's better this way. Let her go with her wahala and then you can be free to hook up with someone casual. You know that's what you need.* The logical voice in his head was insistent.

"See … if you're wondering whether or not I respect you, that has never been an issue. I do and I wouldn't want to make any assumptions about what you want." He should have left it at that, given space for ambiguity. But instead, against his better judgement he went on.

"OK, let's do this then: we go at your pace. We go as far as you want to go, when you want. Is that OK?" Toby could have kicked himself. Since when had he and Adoo become 'we'? He was not ready for a relationship, especially with his issues, let alone with a woman already laden with her own complications. It wasn't even about Zander. It was the fact that having a relationship with her had too much potential for implosion.

And yet Toby felt something inside him awaken, rising to the challenge. He wanted this woman and would use everything in his arsenal to get her. So she was religious? Lots of women were, and it would be up to her to keep that end of her bargain with her Maker.

Toby was about to say bye when he heard someone call out Adoo's name and looked up to see a woman striding purposefully towards them. When she reached them she turned to him, her stare frank and curious. Although she was quite pretty, with high cheekbones, blunt bob haircut, wide eyes and full mouth, he found himself appreciating her beauty in a detached manner.

"Toby, this is Aduke Balogun, my friend, flatmate and business partner," Adoo said.

"Pleasure to meet you," he said. She smiled and cast a playful sideways glance at Adoo.

"Likewise. So, you're the famous Toby that I have been hearing so much about, eh? You're actually as fine as she says you are," she said, tossing her head in Adoo's direction. Adoo's mouth dropped open and Toby laughed, enjoying Adoo's flustered look.

"Aduke! What kind of …" Adoo started to say before Aduke cut her off with a wave of her hand.

"Ehn, stop forming. This is the guy and I'm just meeting him so allow me, jor," she said, turning her attention back at Toby. "I've heard good things about you and I really hope you're treating my friend here nice."

"I'm trying my best – if she would let me. I'm glad to see she has such a caring and concerned friend like you," Toby said, turning on the charm. Aduke raised her eyebrows, smiling.

"And you're charming too? Please do you have any brothers? Single ones, that is."

Toby laughed, answering. "Er … my brother is married and living in Singapore." Aduke looked crestfallen for a moment, but perked up immediately.

"What about cousins?"

"Kai, leave him alone," Adoo said, laughing and reaching up to Toby to take Zander. Zander made a bit of a fuss, refusing to let go of Toby until Toby whispered to him in low tones and he relinquished his hold, his face wreathed in smiles.

"What did you say to him?"

"Oh, let's just say I encouraged him by promising him a treat the next time we meet."

78

"In other words you bribed him. Tau, no problem. So … when are we meeting?" Adoo asked.

"Sometime soon," he said. *Easy there, this is 'Hannani-style' drama waiting to happen, Toby. You're far too scattered where she's concerned. Pull yourself together, man.*

"I look forward to it," she said. He then climbed into his car, and with a slight wave at her and Aduke, he drove off. The ladies stared after him until his car disappeared from sight.

"Nice. Very nice," Aduke murmured.

"Yes indeed," Adoo answered.

\*\*\*

Toby had a busy weekend ahead of him. One of Dare's friends wanted to host a themed bachelor party at The Bar-Rage and Toby was responsible for organising it. This was rather unusual as the club was not used for parties, but Toby thought it would be good to try something new. What made it even better was the fact that he saw it as an opportunity for Adoo and Aduke to take charge of the entire event, which would leave his staff free to serve other guests. He remembered how Adoo had spoken about her love for making cakes and he thought it could work out well. He made the suggestion to Pirfa, the bachelor in question, who readily agreed.

Toby decided to call Adoo with the suggestion. *It's business,* he told himself. *This is what she does and it's a great chance for her to network; I'm not doing this because I want to be around her.*

"See, do you think you and Aduke can handle an event, a bachelor party, to be precise – you know, with all the trimmings like cake and decorations and all that? I know that Pirfa is very specific about a particular theme … I've forgotten what it is exactly but I can arrange for you to meet."

"For sure!" Adoo said. "Just give me his number or arrange a meeting and we can discuss."

On the following Friday afternoon, Aduke and Adoo were putting the finishing touches to the VIP lounge at The Bar-Rage. Pirfa had wanted a PlayStation-themed party and Aduke and Adoo had obliged, setting up video game playing stations around the lounge and creating a holographic-style ambience with the artful use of drapery and lights. The centre had been cleared to create space for dancing and they had also set up serving points for food and drinks in strategic areas around the room. The main attraction was a video game-themed cake, complete with fondant joysticks, control pieces, and multicoloured video game characters. Toby came in and looked around, whistling in appreciation.

"This is great. Well done, you two. I'm really impressed," he said.

Adoo smiled. "Thanks so much. I did my best with what I had but this particular job really made me realise just how much more I need in terms of equipment."

"Oh?" Toby raised his brows.

"Yeah … I need cutters, cake pans, silicone moulds … and there's this crystal chandelier cake stand I'd kill to have … but then I'd have to go to Lagos for all that …" Her eyes had begun to take a faraway look as though her mind was in another place completely, even as she tidied up. Toby cleared his throat.

"Uh … crystal chandelier cake stand?" He had no idea what she was on about.

"Oh, sorry, my mind just ran away with me," she said, chuckling and shaking her head. "I'm finished anyway."

"Are you ready then? Maybe I should take you back home so you can rest a bit and change before the party begins?"

Adoo nodded slowly, a tired smile on her face. He asked Aduke if she needed a lift home but she declined, saying she still needed to do some last-minute checking before heading back home, where she would sleep until the next day.

"So have you been around all day?" Adoo asked him as they drove to her place, her eyes closed as she leaned back fully into the seat.

"No, I came in about an hour ago. Why? Did you miss me?" he asked.

"Nope," she answered. "I was so busy I didn't even notice you weren't there."

"Liar," he whispered. Adoo laughed and reached out to punch his arm lightly. Toby was happy about their easy camaraderie. He also realised that the more his rational mind told him to stay away, the more he felt drawn to her. Something told him that whatever could go wrong, would.

# Eight

"You're sure you won't come? Auntie Jo said she wouldn't mind having Zander for a sleepover with her kids tonight," Adoo said to Aduke. "It's just 6 o'clock and it's not too late for me to take him …" She was trying to convince Aduke to come to the bachelor party they had spent the day organising and setting. But Aduke had refused, volunteering to watch Zander instead.

"Abeg babe … can you just handle this one today? I don't know why, but I am really tired."

"But then, will I be alone?" Adoo asked.

"No, I've asked Sandra to help out today. She owes me a favour and besides, she loves parties. So, she will be there to support you so that you can also spend some time with Toby."

Adoo nodded, relieved to have their mutual friend step in. She knew Sandra well enough to know that she would be up to the task.

"I'll just put on the generator and watch something on MBC. Have fun!" Aduke said.

She shooed Adoo back into her room to get ready before Toby arrived to pick her up. Adoo must have flung every item of clothing she owned around the room before finally settling on an emerald-green bias-cut silk top with a pair of slim-fit denim jeans. She pulled out a pair of leather high-heeled ankle boots she had bought on a whim the year before and put them on, adding a few inches to her petite frame. *Cute but surprisingly comfy. I'll be darned if I'm going to end up with a spinal injury because of some pair of shoes.*

Toby arrived to pick her up sometime after 10pm.

"You look really good, Adoo. But then, you always do," he said, looking her over in admiration. His eyes stopped at her boots. He raised his brows and whistled. "Wow, are you sure you are going to be able to walk in those?"

"My guy, do I look like the kind of woman who would sacrifice comfort? I can walk and even dance azonto in these things!" she said, with mock seriousness as she dismissed him with a wave of her hand. "Besides, seeing as I am challenged in the height department I think these will be a great help to me."

"OK then, just don't break your legs in the process," he said, holding his hands up and feigning surrender.

"The only breaking you'll see is break-dancing," she answered.

Toby laughed. "Break-dancing? Is that a promise?"

"Wait and see," she answered playfully.

By the time they arrived at The Bar-Rage the parking lot was full, with some cars parking in front of others. Toby moved towards his reserved space without a word.

There were a few revellers outside talking loudly and ignoring them as they passed. She could hear the bass from the music in the club even before they entered the foyer. Adoo was overwhelmed as a mixture of cigarette smoke, perfume and sweat hit her. Toby led her towards the VIP lounge. D'Banj's 'Oliver Twist' was playing at an eardrum-bursting level and the party was in full swing judging from the number of people on the dance floor. Others were standing on by the sidelines, shouting at each other.

Adoo noticed a few young men playing video games on the side and a few people taking pictures with a man who was standing next to the cake, presumably the groom-to-be. She saw some of those with him gesturing at the cake and making comments about how beautiful and well made it was; some even took out their phones and cameras to take pictures. Toby put his hand lightly on her back and she looked up at him and he smiled.

"Let me introduce you to Pirfa."

Adoo grinned, happy to finally meet him in person as they had coordinated all the party plans over the phone. Pirfa enveloped her hand in his and flashed her his warm smile.

"It's so good to finally meet the person responsible for this wonderful event," he said, gesturing towards the hall. I am really impressed. Thank you!"

Adoo beamed, feeling a sense of pride at her and Aduke's achievments.

Then he capped it by looking at Toby and saying, "I don't know where you found this lady, but she's an asset to you. You'd better not let her go."

"I don't intend to," Toby replied. Adoo looked up at him but his eyes were still on Pirfa. She was confused by his cryptic response. Was she an asset to him purely in business terms … or otherwise?

She didn't get the chance to clarify that as Toby excused himself and Adoo nodded. Pirfa also gave his excuses and left her standing next to the cake. She began to move away slowly, not knowing where exactly to go. She threw her shoulders back, determined to mingle.

She didn't have to wait very long as a young man soon found his way to her side. Before long they were having an animated conversation about politics and business in Nigeria. They moved towards the drinks section and Adoo took a Coke while Tunde, her new discussion partner, poured himself something a little stronger. They resumed their talk and Tunde moved on to more personal matters.

"I really like you, Adoo," he said, licking his lips and scanning her from head to toe. She felt uncomfortable at his perusal and wondered how to change the subject. Then he leaned towards her, too close for comfort. "I think you are my type of woman."

She kept a diplomatic smile on her face, while calculating the best way to put some distance between them without seeming prudish or rude. *Oh, why does the one person I decide to talk to have to try to toast me?*

Tunde continued, "I'd like to get to know you a bit better. Maybe we could talk outside in my car, where there is less noise and more privacy?" The way he said 'privacy' sent shivers down Adoo's spine.

"Er … I don't think that's a good idea. I think we can continue our conversation comfortably here," she said, taking a small step back, still smiling. He came closer.

"Why na? Are you afraid of me? Or do you have a boyfriend?"

She was about to open her mouth and tell him in no uncertain terms that she was not interested in him and did not need to answer his questions when she felt hands on either side of her waist. She gasped in shock, turned quickly and found herself facing an amused Toby. She almost chided him for scaring her when he cut her off, speaking directly to her in a voice loud enough for Tunde to hear.

"Eh-hehn! I've been looking all over for you. See, even in these heels you're still smaller than everyone else and hard to find in a crowd." She narrowed her eyes at him but he ignored her and swiftly turned his attention from her to Tunde, who had a confused look on his face. "Hello, I'm Toby. It's nice to meet you. And you are?" Toby extended his right hand towards Tunde while keeping his other hand on Adoo's waist.

A look of understanding settled on Tunde's face as he shook Toby's hand and introduced himself. After making some small talk he said a very proper 'bye-bye' to Adoo, and was on his way, leaving Adoo and Toby alone.

"Now that was fun," Toby said. He was still holding

her waist, and looked down at her with a gleam in his eye and a playful smile on his lips. "I saw you a while back and you should have seen the look on your face. You looked like you were trying desperately to dodge the guy."

"And you just had to come over and save me, eh?" she said, smiling wryly, pinning him down with her eyes. "I don't need protection or saving, Toby. You didn't exactly have to do the whole territorial thing there. I would have handled it well o!"

He opened his mouth and for a moment she thought he wanted to say something but instead he just exhaled and nodded. She smiled and let him introduce her to a few people he knew. Toby excused himself again to use the restroom.

Not five minutes after he left Adoo heard a man say behind her, "Hannani? Hannani, is that you?"

Perplexed, she turned around and saw a man she didn't recognise looking intently at her. *Oh no, not another unwanted toaster,* she thought to herself. *But ... why had he called her Hannani?* She remembered Toby mentioning that the girl he'd been hurt by was called Hannani and wondered if this guy was talking about the same woman. The man squinted at her before speaking again.

"Oh, I'm sorry, I don't mean to be rude. It's just that you look just like an old friend of mine. The resemblance is quite striking, except that you're darker. But everything else is the same: the height, build, and even the glasses!"

"Really? That's interesting …" Adoo said, letting the sentence hang to encourage him to say more. She felt awkward but wanted to hear more about this mysterious Hannani. He obliged, smiling and offering his hand to shake, which she took.

"By the way, I'm Gerald. And you are …?"

"Adoo. Please do tell me more about this Hannani. I'm really interested to know about my twin." she said, attempting to make her voice light and tipping her head to the side. Before Gerald could say more she heard Toby's voice from behind her.

"Ah-ah? Gerald? Geraldo? Is that you?" Shock and delight spread across Gerald's face as he looked beyond her. She turned to see Toby coming to meet them. The two men pumped hands furiously, like old friends glad to see each other. Adoo was sure then that the Hannani Gerald had mistaken her for was Toby's Hannani.

"Na wa o!" Gerald exclaimed. "So this is where you ended up? J-town? Can you see this life? Wetin you dey do here?"

"I run this club," Toby answered. "You sef, wetin you dey do for dis town?"

"Pirfa and I are friends and I'm here to attend his wedding tomorrow. From the way this party dey rock I hope he will make it to his own wedding … sober." They both laughed. Gerald then turned his attention to Adoo, who was watching the whole thing, a little bemused.

"Toby, I was just telling Adoo here how much she resembles Hannani! You remember Hannani, don't you? Oh, what am I saying? Of course you remember her. You guys were tight back then. In fact, a lot of us thought you two were cutting shows, at least before she and Bala got engaged." Adoo saw Toby wince at the direction the conversation was taking. Gerald took no notice however, and continued talking.

"Do you know, if it wasn't for the fact that Hannani is fairer, I would have sworn Adoo was her? They even tip their heads the same way, you know," he said, turning to Toby who now had an uncomfortable expression on his face. "Abi na lie I dey lie, guy?"

Adoo felt herself grow cold, realisation and mortification filling her. "So … basically Hannani and I are almost like twins, eh?" she asked Gerald. She smiled coldly, her voice like granite. "The similarities are that many? With almost no differences between us, abi?"

"Truly, you are just like her," Gerald said smiling, oblivious to Toby's silent entreaties for him to keep quiet and Adoo's growing fury. Then he turned to Toby and delivered the coup de grâce. "You know, all of us wondered why the two of you didn't just get together before she even started going out with Bala. Me sha, I thought you were a perfect match and letting her go was … Anyway, na so life be. So, Toby, you get babe for J-town?"

But Toby didn't answer. Instead his hands were on his hips and his eyes cast downwards.

Adoo turned to Toby, with a wide smile pasted on her face. "Na true o Toby, you get babe for J-town, sef? E be like say dis Hannani woman go give your babe serious assignment." Despite her smile, Adoo felt a deep sense of mortification. The very idea that she was a mannequin replacement for someone else in Toby's life hurt her deeply.

Gerald looked from Adoo to Toby, then back again, looking uncomfortable. He opened his mouth to say something but Adoo cut him off.

"Gerald, it was a real pleasure meeting you and I hope you enjoy the wedding tomorrow," she said in the most dignified and diplomatic tone she could manage. "I have a bit of a headache and I think I need to be getting home now. I hope we meet again sometime." Gerald looked at a loss for words. He swallowed and nodded, stealing glances at Toby, whose eyes were fixed on Adoo.

She turned and walked out of the VIP lounge with all its noise and gaiety, out of the main hall and into the open. The fresh air hit her in a wave, the cold wrapping around her and giving her skin goose bumps. She wrapped her arms around herself to ward off the biting chill, her teeth chattering. Much worse than the cold nipping at her flesh on the outside was the frost gathering around her heart.

She brought out her phone to call Sandra. After a few rings, Sandra picked and Adoo could hear the noise in the background.

"Adoo, what's up?"

"Sandra, I'm ... er ... not feeling too well and I think I

need to go home. I know I shouldn't be dumping all this on you, but, can you just hold the fort ... see to it that everything goes well tonight?"

"You're sick? Kai, sorry my dear ... don't worry I have got your back."

"Adoo bit her lip, cringing at the lie she was telling. "Something like that. Listen, you don't have to do anything much; just let them leave everything as it is and Aduke and I will come in the morning to sort it out. I'm sure I'll feel better by then."

"No problem at all, Adoo. I hope you do feel better ..."

Adoo closed her eyes, swallowing a lump in her throat before answering with a quiet, "I hope so too. Thank you so much, Sandra."

Just as she hung up she heard footsteps behind her and Toby calling her name.

She bit her lip, willing herself to keep calm and not cry in front of him. She turned and fixed a rigid stare on him.

"Adoo, where are you going? What's up with you?"

"I don't know, Toby. You tell me. Maybe it's the smoke and the noise affecting me. Or maybe it's the fact that I have just realised that the only reason you ever gave me face is because I happen to be a clone of your ex-girlfriend," she said, her voice dripping sarcasm. "Since you couldn't have the real thing you decided to find a substitute. Tokunbo. Okrika. A carbon copy.

Toby narrowed his eyes. "And you came to that conclusion based on what a complete stranger said?"

"You'd be shocked at how honest people who don't know you can be, simply because they have nothing to hide," she retorted.

Toby's face creased into a frown. "Now you're being unreasonable, Adoo. And you're shivering from the cold so why don't we get into the car and talk?"

"I don't want to talk to you," she said, unable to keep the petulant tone out of her voice.

Tony exhaled in exasperation. "Fine then, don't talk to me but at least get yourself out of the cold so you don't die of pneumonia."

Adoo stood stubbornly for a moment and it seemed that the wind whistled a little faster and the temperature dropped lower in that split second. A couple stumbled out of the club, the female very drunk and the guy only slightly less so. They staggered past Adoo, the girl giggling and the guy crooning into her ear as they headed towards one of the cars. She turned her attention back on Toby, who stood calmly regarding her. *And he's got a nice warm sweater on, curse him!* she seethed.

Everything in her wanted to refuse any form of contact or aid from Toby but practicality conquered emotion. She started to walk towards his car, wishing she had her old clunker Bunny to take her home. She would rather have chugged and lurched all the way back to Rantya than endure one minute in the warmth and luxury of Toby's Mercedes. He opened the door and she slid into the passenger seat. He got in and closed the door, then started the car but didn't put it in gear. She kept her face stony and stared straight ahead. He started to say something but stopped, clearly unsure of what to say. Adoo didn't give him time to gather his thoughts.

"Can you please take me back home?" she said, her voice devoid of emotion. Toby sighed and began to reverse. Before long they were on their way back to Rantya. Neither of them spoke all the way back, as Adoo stared out of the window at the lights.

They reached the gate to the estate and, as Adoo made a move to leave the car. Toby spoke.

"Adoo, I have never tried to substitute you for Hannani. Why would I do that? I'll admit that at first you reminded me of her but ..." Adoo waited for him to say more. When he didn't she sighed and spoke with resignation in her voice.

"Look Toby, I am tired. Na gaji. I am tired of never being enough and I am tired of being compared to other people. Now I understand what your ... pull to me was. It was her all along, wasn't it?"

"Oh, come on, Adoo," he said calmly, but Adoo thought his tone was patronising, as though he was trying to quiet a child. Irritation flooded her and she cut him off before he could say more.

"So you were thinking of her when you were kissing me, right? And that time in your house, was it to try and relive your experience with her?"

Toby kept silent. Adoo shook her head and spoke again.

"Look, I really don't want to talk about it any more.

But I'll say thank you: thank you for being so nice to my son, for all you've done, for being a nice guy. But I'm done with that. Zander and I will be fine on our own. I wish you the very best in life. Goodbye."

With that she leaped out of the car and marched into the compound. As she walked in a part of her hoped he would come in after her and try to clear things up. She wanted him to say something, anything, to reassure her that he wanted to be with her and her alone. Then she heard the car starting up and the unmistakable sound of tyres on gravel as he drove away. The disappointment was so acute she could taste it at the back of her tongue. She swallowed hard, willing herself not to shed any tears.

\*\*\*

Aduke patted Adoo's back as she cried, her heaving sobs coming out muted for fear of waking Zander up. Her make-up was all over her face and her hair was a mess. She had stumbled into the flat, taking off her shoes and casting them off in a careless heap on the floor, with Aduke looking at her incredulously.

"Stupid shoes. Why did I wear them?" Adoo said before bursting into tears, leaving Aduke bewildered and confused.

"You're crying because of the shoes?" Aduke asked.

"Men are horrible. God punish all of them," Adoo had sobbed. Aduke made her sit down and now was letting her cry, rubbing her back and crooning softly to try to calm her down. After a while, when Adoo calmed down to occasional sniffles, Aduke went to the kitchen and emerged with a steaming mug of Ovaltine. She handed it to Adoo, who took it gratefully, taking tentative sips. Aduke leaned back against the sofa, and waited for Adoo to speak when she was ready.

"I don't understand why I never seem to be enough for the men who come into my life," she said, looking down into the mug. Aduke said nothing and Adoo continued. "All this time I thought he really liked being around me but it turns out he was just using me to replace someone else."

"You mean Toby?" Aduke asked. "How is that?"

"It turns out I'm a replica of the woman he once loved who didn't feel the same about him. He carried around that broken heart until he found someone who reminded him of her: me. It's like this Hannani has haunted me from the day Toby and I met."

"Hannani?" Aduke shook her head, not following.

"Oh, you don't know. Let me tell you then." Adoo proceeded to narrate the events of the evening to Aduke, taking care to mention the connection between her, Hannani and Toby. Aduke clucked sympathetically but otherwise kept her comments to herself as Adoo spoke.

"Well?" Adoo asked, sniffling.

"Tau... I really don't know what to say, DooDoo," she said, using her old nickname for Adoo. "It's not as if you were in a relationship, per se, and the man didn't make any promises."

"I know, Aduke," she sniffed. "But it still hurts to think that while I thought we had a good friendship going he obviously felt differently."

"I think you need to give yourself a bit of time to think things through, sha. I also think you should give him a chance to explain himself. Just because you look like this Hannani woman doesn't necessarily mean he's using you to replace her. In all the time you've spent with him has he ever given you reason to think that way?"

"I … I just don't want to get hurt again, Aduke," she said quietly.

"You can't avoid being hurt in life … and you know how insensitive men can be. I think you should hear him out, eh?"

"Well, I agree with you on one thing … Anyway, I need sleep," Adoo said, yawning and stretching as she stood. "I'll think more clearly in the morning. Thanks, sweetie."

"As for those ridiculous shoes," Aduke called out with an impish smile on her face. "I sure say you rocked dem die, sha. No be small ting."

Adoo kissed her teeth and shook her head, a smile on her face as they both went to their rooms.

Adoo woke up to the sound of Saturday morning cartoons and the smell of stew wafting in through her open door. She lay back in bed, uttering a prayer of thanks for being able to fall asleep with relative ease after her discussion with Aduke. Then she remembered Toby and resisted the overwhelming urge to pick up the phone and hear his voice. And with the recollection of his voice came images of him, his eyes and the way the edges crinkled when he smiled, the slight inflection of his voice when he chuckled. How she loved his voice. How she loved him.

*Eh? Love ke? You love him? Why?* she asked herself, realising the answer before she gasped. She was in love with him. She didn't know when it had happened but it had. And what a time to realise it, just after she had walked away from him. She groaned and turned her head to the pillow, punching it with fists and screamed, the sound muffled by the foam. What on earth was she supposed to do about that now? Her warm, fuzzy feelings didn't change the cold, hard fact that whatever Toby wanted with her was simply a superimposition of what he had wanted for him and Hannani.

Adoo swore under her breath, something she rarely did, as she turned over to stare at the ceiling. *Pull yourself together woman,* she chided herself. *You clean up and you move on. You've done it before.* But this was different. She couldn't remember Teremun ever treating her like a lady, respecting her and actually listening to her. She sighed as she reluctantly got up from her bed.

She plodded past the living room, where Zander lay on the couch watching TV and went straight to the dining area, where Aduke sat at the table with a delectable-looking sandwich on her plate. Adoo swooped in and grabbed one half of the sandwich, biting into it before Aduke had time to protest.

"Good morning to you too … and thank you for stealing my breakfast," Aduke said. Adoo responded by sticking her tongue out at her.

"You seem better this morning," Aduke said.

Adoo smiled, although she felt as though her heart was bruised. "Maybe all this is a sign that I'm not meant to be with any man. They all seem to bring problems anyway. And I really don't need it. All I want is peace." Aduke shrugged as she ate.

***

The call came just after Adoo had finished with choir practice in preparation for Sunday service. She had stopped to talk to some of the other choir members and was holding Zander's hand when her phone rang. She looked at the screen and saw an unfamiliar number. She frowned, wondering who it was, but decided to answer.

"Hello?"

"Hmmm … you still sound the same, DooDoo," a male voice drawled. Her hands suddenly went cold and clammy and she tightened her grip on Zander's hand. He began to fidget in discomfort, whining until she loosened her grip.

"Teremun?"

A soft, sinister laugh confirmed her worst fears. "I was starting to wonder if you had forgotten me. But I'm sure you remember every detail about me, don't you?" Adoo found her skin crawling as she remembered his cold, snake-like eyes. She wondered for the millionth time what she had ever seen in an opportunistic lecher like Teremun.

"Where did you get my number?" she demanded.

"Ah-ah? You dey vex so? Yes, I remember you always having a temper. Anyway this is Naija so getting your number isn't a problem. All I had to do was ask the right people."

"What do you want, Teremun?" she snapped. She had no patience with this juvenile game.

"I want what's mine, Adoo. I want my son."

# Nine

Toby had switched off his phone as soon as he got back home the previous evening. He'd been in no mood for any distractions. He hadn't even bothered to put on the lights in the house, just turning on the outside security lights before going upstairs to his room. He had undressed and collapsed on his bed, too tired to do anything else. Going to bed in a foul mood, he was in an even fouler mood in the morning.

*Women and their damned habit of jumping to the wrong conclusions,* he seethed the next morning. He would never understand them as long as he lived. He got up, brushed his teeth and shaved, then went downstairs and turned on the TV to a news station. As the newscaster droned on in the background, he made a quick breakfast and turned on his phone to write a text to his assistant informing him that he would not be coming in to work that day. As soon as there was confirmation that the message had been delivered he switched off his phone again.

He willed himself not to brood and tried to peptalk himself into feeling better than he did.

*Well, you didn't want to get tangled up in any messy business and now she doesn't want to talk to you.* He tried to shake the voice from his head but he couldn't. Maybe his insomnia was messing up his head. *You should be happy that all that potential drama just walked out of your life, man. No complications. No potential Hannani-style disasters. Just goodbye.* It all sounded so logical and surgical in his mind. He should be heaving a great sigh of relief and rejoicing in his freedom. Then why did he feel like he had messed up something that could have been so good? How long would he allow his past to affect his future? Adoo was not Hannani.

He went over her accusations again. "*Since you couldn't have the real thing you decided to get a substitute. Tokunbo. Okrika,*" she had said.

He honestly didn't think it was like that. Yes, there were plenty of similarities between her and Hannani and perhaps that was what had drawn him to her in the beginning; that much he could admit. But then Adoo was in a class of her own, and she was not someone to be easily replaced or used as a substitute. Toby also realised that, as time passed and he spent more time with Adoo and got to know her, the memory of Hannani had begun to fade and seem less appealing.

That was it! He would give her time to cool off and then try to talk to her. He wouldn't make any promises but at least he would be more open to letting go of the past.

With a smile on his face he took his sandwich and coffee and plopped down on the couch in front of the TV, determined to enjoy his day off from work and hoping that on the other side of town, Adoo was also taking time to cool off.

Toby thought about going to see Adoo the next day but he held back, knowing that she had been deeply hurt by what had happened at the party at The Bar-Rage and would probably not want to talk to him too soon. He decided to wait a few days before going to see her to iron things out.

He had finally admitted to himself that, despite all the inner warnings, he had grown to care for Adoo a little more than he should. He knew that they might not recover their easy-going friendship but he was willing to try. He missed her greatly and wanted to take the next step, regardless of what might go wrong.

He agonised over what to do, thinking about the usual token of flowers and chocolates designed to soften the heart of a female but, somehow, none of them seemed adequate to convey the depth of his feelings for Adoo. Admitting his desire to go deep into a relationship with Adoo was an unknown pool and, though he had some trepidation, he was willing to dive into it.

He picked up the phone several times and started to call but then cut it off before it began to ring. As juvenile as the action seemed, he realised that he was actually afraid of the outcome. What if she totally rejected him? What if the hurt caused by the night at the club had cut too deep and she was unwilling to let it go? That was a possible conclusion he didn't really want to think about.

\*\*\*

A few days had passed since the phone call from Teremun and Adoo's mind had been in a whirl. She had to admit that she was afraid, not wanting to lose her son but also not wanting to show her fear openly. As she piped a butter cream border onto a birthday cake on the dining table, she went over the conversation again, every excruciating word.

"I want what's mine, Adoo. I want my son."

Her body had grown hot and cold at the same time. She couldn't breathe. "What are you talking about?" she had whispered.

"Stop pretending! Were you not pregnant when we split up?"

"We didn't 'split up', Teremun. You left me. You abandoned me when I was almost six months pregnant. As for my son, do you even know his name?"

Teremun made an impatient sound. "Look, all this long English you're speaking doesn't mean anything. The boy is my son and I want him," he had said. "I'll send the police to collect him if I have to. You're not the only one with money and connections now."

"Come and get him if you think you can, you disgusting …"

Teremun had laughed and Adoo had the overwhelming urge to reach into the phone and slap the smirk she was sure was on his face.

"You have never been a part of his life and you won't force your way into it now, Teremun. You have no legal right to him and a court will prove it."

"Court, eh? In fact that will be even better. This is Nigeria, Adoo, and you know very well that here children belong to their fathers. There is no law – traditional or otherwise – that will not hand him over to me. And if you try and make it difficult for me, I'll make sure I get him by force. You'll be hearing from me …" With that he had hung up.

Adoo shuddered as she remembered the conversation. She had thought long and hard about what to do. She would need legal counsel – that was for sure. She was thankful that she had stashed away a reasonable amount in one of her savings accounts, but this was a storm of unimaginable proportions.

It was already after 4pm and Zander was home from school, sprawled on the living room rug playing with Lego. Aduke had called to say she would be held up a little in town. Adoo had just put the piping bag down and was about to sprinkle nonpareils on the cake when she heard the sound of arguing at the far side of the compound, near the gate.

She walked to the window and pulled back the curtain and her blood froze. It was the mai-guard shouting and gesturing at Teremun. *He had found her!*

She took a deep breath and went to the kitchen to rinse her hands. Then she walked towards the door, telling Zander to stay put as she went out to face her one-time love and present-day nemesis.

***

Toby couldn't put it off any longer: he had to go and see Adoo and explain things. He didn't expect anything, but he hoped that she would at least listen to him.

He drove towards Rantya, listening to music and trying to clear his mind, feeling that the best way to speak would be unrehearsed. As he drew near, he noticed a shiny navy blue BMW parked a few metres from the gate. His brow furrowed, wondering why the mai-guard had not asked the owner of the car to park in a better way. The gate had also been left open, as though someone had walked in, which was unusual. He stopped his car and got out, walking towards Adoo's flat.

She was standing in front of her flat, her arms crossed as she glared at a man. The man's back was turned to Toby so he couldn't see his face. He slowed his pace a little, not wanting to interrupt Adoo's conversation.

She said something and shook her head vehemently and the man gestured towards the flat. She shook her head again and took a step back. Then the man reached out and grabbed her arm hard.

Toby felt his senses kick into gear as he hurried towards them. He put a hand on the man's shoulder.

"There is no need for you to lay your hands on her that way," he said quietly, a dangerous edge to his voice. Adoo looked at Toby with sparks in her eyes, her jaws tensed, and then looked defiantly back at the man. He turned around and Toby got a good look at him.

He was good-looking in a generic way, with well-shaped features. Toby could also read weakness and petulance in his weak chin and expression. This was a man who clearly intimidated only those whom he was strong enough to bully. Unfortunately for him, Toby was not one of those.

"Who the hell are you?" he snarled at Toby, shaking off his hand. Toby ignored him and looked at Adoo.

"You OK?"

"I'm fine," she said irritably and Toby frowned, wondering why she was reacting to him that way. She continued, with a dismissive wave of her hand. "This is Teremun."

*Oh. Ex-boyfriend and 'baby daddy'. Best to tread lightly.*

"He was just about to leave," she said.

"Leave ke? I want my son. Where is he?" he growled. Toby was at a loss for what to do. He didn't want to involve himself in what was clearly Adoo's personal business but he didn't want to leave her alone with a man who clearly had no sense of physical restraint around her.

"If you want him, you will have to try to get him in court," she said, drawing herself up, her back ramrod straight as she looked him directly in the eye. At that moment, Zander poked his head out of the door.

"Mummy? Mummy, will you come inside?" His innocent voice jarred with the strained atmosphere.

Teremun turned and looked at Zander, smirking. "So that's him, eh? Fine-looking boy."

Zander looked at Teremun with curiosity. "Mummy, who is this?"

"Go inside, Zander," she answered firmly, her eyes never leaving Teremun's.

"Oh, the boy doesn't know he has a father? Or have you confused him by bringing a parade of 'uncles' around?" he said slyly. Adoo closed her eyes briefly and Toby felt the rage rising and clenched his fists at his sides, willing himself not to wipe the leer off Teremun's face by force. Zander stayed outside, curiosity overriding obedience.

"Mummy?"

"I said 'Go inside, Zander,'" she repeated, this time with a harsh edge to her voice. Teremun started to move past her towards Zander and she brought up her hands and caught his chest, pushing him away. He lost his balance briefly and, when he regained it, Toby saw a look of utter malice cross his face as he moved towards Adoo. Before anybody could react, Teremun had grabbed Adoo and shoved her violently out of the way, causing her to stumble and fell to her knees. He then made to walk past her towards Zander, who had begun to whimper, his eyes wide open in fright.

Toby reacted on instinct, clenching his fist as he spun Teremun around and punched him across his jaw. The impact was hard enough to send him reeling. Toby didn't take his eyes off him, drawing himself up to his full height, his breathing coming in puffs. He didn't look at Adoo as he asked her if she was OK.

Teremun regained his composure and brought a finger to his bleeding lip, narrowing his eyes at Toby.

"Oh, so you're her bodyguard now, eh? I'm sure you have other ... duties," he said, goading Toby. Toby felt Adoo's hand on his arm as she spoke.

"Stop right now, Toby."

She positioned herself in front of Toby, facing Teremun squarely. "Get out, Teremun. Like I said earlier: if you want Zander you will have to face me in court. Until then, if you come near me again I will make it a police case."

"Police? They won't do anything once they know you prevented me from seeing my son and even had your boyfriend beat me up," he spat. Toby took a step towards him but Adoo held him back.

"Toby, don't make this even worse than it already is."

Toby felt himself chafe at her reprimand. How exactly had he made anything worse? He had come to try to make peace and had found himself in the middle of a war instead. Teremun laughed.

"Aaw, that's so sweet. She can even make you stand down, eh? Be very careful with this one o, she's extremely fertile. You'd knock her up in one try." Then Teremun proceeded to describe Toby's relationship with Adoo in such a vulgar way it made her gasp. Toby kept his cool. Teremun shrugged.

"You want this to reach court, eh? OK then, I'll give you court. See you then. Oh, and make sure I don't see Mr Bodyguard around or I will make things even harder for you legally than you can imagine." With that he turned and stormed off, not looking back as he left the compound, walking past the confused mai-guard who had stood quietly at the gate through the entire ordeal. A few seconds later they heard the car door bang shut, and the engine revved as Teremun sped away.

Dusk was beginning to set in and Toby turned to see one of Adoo's neighbours peeping through her curtains, probably having witnessed the scene. He glowered at her and she quickly dropped the curtain.

Adoo walked over to Zander, holding him and comforting him as he held on to her.

"Adoo, I … I just wanted to …" he began. She cut him off, looking at him with eyes that glistened with tears. Those tears were almost his undoing and he wanted to wipe them away. Something in her stance told him to keep his distance, though.

"Please, Toby … please just leave. I can't take any more today, OK? Please just go," she whispered.

Toby could do nothing but nod as he turned, leaving her with Zander. As he got into his car and drove off, he wondered if he would ever get the chance to make things right with Adoo.

*\*\**

"Auntie, I really need your help," Adoo said, controlling herself lest her emotions got the better of her and she began to bawl on the phone. She was speaking to her parents' longtime friend and her godmother, Barrister Benita Oyebade. Auntie Benita was a lawyer who specialised in industrial and property matters. But Adoo was quite sure she would know of a lawyer who could handle custody cases. She was also a dear aunt, an older lady Adoo looked up to, who had helped her when her own parents had chosen to step back. She was objective and honest to the point of bluntness, but she had a kind heart and soft spot for Adoo.

Adoo knew that though it would have been more prudent for her to have gone to her parents for help, she needed to fight for her son on her own and on her terms. She'd had a strained relationship with her parents ever since she moved in with Teremun and got pregnant. She supposed she couldn't blame them for being disappointed. She hoped that at some point they would be fully reconciled. However, right now she needed to focus her energy on fighting for Zander.

"Tell me about the case," Auntie Benita said in her clipped English accent. Adoo told her everything from Teremun's call to his visit, taking care to minimise Toby's role except for the part where he hit Teremun. After she finished Auntie Benita spoke.

"Technically I would say he has no legal claim on the child but a good lawyer can argue otherwise. If you don't respond with wise legal counsel then you may have problems."

"And he chooses to wait all this time to play the concerned father," Adoo responded.

"It's ridiculous," Auntie Benita said, clicking her tongue in disapproval. "Now, eh, you mentioned that your friend, Toby, hit him when he came over? That might prove to be an issue as this Teremun creature can make it out to be that he was attacked without provocation. As far as the case is concerned, I would advise that Mr Toby remain as far away from Teremun as possible to avoid complications."

Adoo mulled that over before continuing.

"Auntie, I need proper legal counsel. And I need the best. You've been a lawyer for *ages* … er, no offence," she said at Auntie's harrumph.

"Well, I shall be travelling to Abuja in a few days. I happen to know an excellent lawyer who deals in such matters so I'll give him a call. I will get back to you on that as soon as I can," she said. Adoo smiled and nodded, hoping that she would be able to afford whoever Auntie Benita recommended. No matter; even if she had to take a loan for lawyer's fees, she would. Zander was worth it.

"And now, my dear, on to other important matters," she said, in low and knowing tone. Adoo sat up a little straighter in her chair, gripping the phone tightly and steeling herself for the inevitable questions that she was sure would cut to the core: Aunty Benita was incredibly perceptive.

"There is something else bothering you, something other than this looming battle for your son, I believe," she said, getting no denials from Adoo. "My instinct tells that there is a man involved. And not that idiot he-goat you call the father of your son. And I have a feeling it's this Toby friend of yours, isn't it?" Adoo thought Auntie Benita could be downright theatrical when she got into her confession-extraction mode and had to stifle a sigh.

Adoo kept silent, afraid to speak lest she reveal too much. Toby had been constantly on her mind since she had last seen him a few days ago. But with all she had to deal with she had to force herself to place him on the back burner, waiting to be brought out and dealt with at a later, more convenient time. It would seem Aunty Benita was forcing her to bring him out and blow the dust off the issue.

"Auntie, you've always been able to read me too easily," she said. Auntie Benita clucked her tongue.

"And?"

"It's complicated, Auntie," she said. Auntie Benita exhaled loudly.

"Nothing with men is truly complicated, when you think about it. Either want him or you don't. Either he wants you or he doesn't."

"It's not that simple …" Adoo said weakly. Auntie Benita cut her off.

"Why not? If he cares for you and your son then there is no reason for you not to pursue a relationship. Are you trying to punish yourself for being a single mother by convincing yourself that you cannot be happy with any other man?"

"He loves someone else, Auntie," Adoo said with an air of defeated finality.

"And did he tell you this?" Auntie Benita was relentless, determined to bare Adoo's heart and dissect it with her cutting pragmatism. "If not, I see no need for you to convince yourself otherwise."

When they had ended their conversation, Adoo sat for a while, thinking. She wanted to call Toby and apologise but didn't quite know what to say. Then she got an idea. She smiled, got up and set to work, even though it was already 10pm at night and both Aduke and Zander were fast asleep.

*** 

The following day, Adoo set off to drop Zander at school with a smile on her face. She had a purpose and not even the horrible morning traffic would sway her or spoil her mood. She slipped a *Veggie Tales* CD into her sound system and found herself singing along, competing with Zander on the decibel level.

By the time she dropped him off, he was giggling uncontrollably and he hugged her tightly before she left. As she drove off she glanced at the cake box behind, a New York-style strawberry cheesecake she had baked for Toby as a peace offering, remembering that he had mentioned in one of their conversations that it was one of his favourite desserts. She would drop it off at his office and then try to meet up with him later in the day so they could talk.

She went to The Bar-Rage, handed the box to one of the waiters – Selbol, as his name tag read – and instructed him to keep it in the fridge until Toby arrived. She left with a grin, looking forward to seeing him.

That afternoon, at about 4pm, Adoo was at home when her phone rang. She answered to the voice of a furious female on the other end.

"What poison did you put in that thing you sent to Oga?" the lady snarled, and she recognised the voice as that of Emem, the hostess at The Bar-Rage. Confusion racked her mind as she thought, *Poison? What?*

"I don't know what you're talking about," she said.

Emem made a disbelieving sound. "You don't know, eh? They had to take him to the hospital because he got very sick after he ate some of that stuff you sent."

Adoo shook her head as she answered. "I don't understand. How is he sick? How did that happen?" she asked, worry flooding her.

"See, all I know is that he ate that thing and not long after he started to vomit all over his office and had to be taken to the hospital. What did you put in it?"

"I don't … wait. Where is the guy I gave it to, one Selbol? I told him to put it in the fridge immediately. Did he do it?" Adoo asked insistently. She heard muffled voices in the background, and then shouting. Then Emem was back on the line.

"He said he forgot to put it in the fridge immediately and only remembered about thirty minutes before Oga came."

Adoo closed her eyes, realising that Toby had probably suffered from an acute attack of food poisoning. Cheesecake could quickly become a breeding ground for bacteria if not kept cool. She exhaled and asked, "Which hospital is he in?"

\*\*\*

Toby was sitting on his hospital bed with his legs over the edge and an I.V. tube stuck in his hand when she walked in. She felt a wave of guilt hit her as he looked at her and she saw his ashen face. He smiled weakly at her as she walked in.

"I've heard of 'Death by Chocolate' ... but cheesecake?" he joked. She shook her head.

"Toby, I'm so sorry. I didn't ... I gave strict instructions to ..."

"I know," he answered, his voice a little subdued. "It was all just a mistake. And, rabid food poisoning aside, I really appreciate the gesture."

She sat down on the only cushion provided in the stark room, looking at him. He shook his head and said, "Well, this is rather embarrassing, actually. Here I was trying to form hero and then I end up throwing up rather colourfully in my office. Now I'm sitting here in this ugly hospital room like a wet rag in front of you. So not cool."

She laughed, feeling herself melt all the more in his presence. She looked around, taking in the environment. He was right: the room really was ugly with limp blue curtains, a metal frame bed, grey terrazzo tiles on the floors and walls painted a shade between cream and yellow. A tattered mosquito net was suspended above the bed with thin, stretched yarn and there was a strong smell of Izal disinfectant and insect repellent.

He spoke again. "Adoo, about that day with … that guy. I'm sorry, not about hitting him as such, but doing it in front of Zander and maybe making things more difficult for you in the long run."

"It's okay, Toby. I know you only wanted to defend me and I appreciate that but … well, this is a battle I have to fight …"

"For yourself. I know," he said with an air of finality. "I'll keep my distance until it's all sorted out."

She didn't know what to say. Then the phone rang. It was Auntie Benita.

"Adoo, darling, it seems I have to run to England to attend a conference I had promised to be a guest speaker at. I could have sworn I wrote it down somewhere … I wonder where I left that blasted diary …" she murmured, almost to herself. Adoo chuckled and rolled her eyes: trust Auntie Benita to forget where she put her diary. The lady had been known to 'forget' her glasses as they sat on her head!

"Okay Auntie," she answered, letting the conversation be led by the affable lady at the other end.

"Yes, yes … er … but I'll call my lawyer friend when I get there and get back to you, alright?"

When the conversation ended, Adoo let out a sigh.

"Are you OK?" Toby asked.

"Well, my auntie who promised to help me get a lawyer to handle my case has to go to England and I'm hoping she can make the connection for me before it's too late."

"You need a lawyer ..." Toby said, letting the sentence trail away, as he looked to the side, as though thinking of something.

"Yep, and I need one quick," she said. Then she looked at her watch and gasped. "Oh my goodness, I have to go and pick Zander up now!"

She leaned over to kiss him on his cheek but, in a split instant, whether by chance or design, he turned his head and her lips brushed his. She drew back, unsure of what to say and he looked at her, as though expecting her to speak. All the words she had in her head dissolved, as though they had flown out of her ears and left her with nothing. She wasn't even sure there were any right words. She steadied herself, uttered a soft 'Take care, Toby' and walked out, leaving him sitting on his hospital bed. She noticed that he had a pensive look on his face.

\*\*\*

Toby sat on his bed, thinking about the woman who had just left. He cared about her more than she knew but circumstances meant that he couldn't tell her about his feelings without complicating her life even further. The way she blew hot and cold wasn't helping matters either: he had seen how she clammed up after kissing him in his kitchen and he didn't want to push.

She had opened up to him and let him know of the betrayal and rejection she had suffered at Teremun's hands. And, instead of going to her place to make things better, he had managed to make them worse. He sighed, wondering if things would ever be the same between them and if there was a chance to move forward. He could have sworn that he had seen something in her eyes earlier on that could give him hope. But he decided that, if she felt something for him, she would have to admit it. He would not coax it out of her. He was patient; he could wait it out.

Then a thought occurred to him. And an idea began to take root in his mind.

# Ten

Just two days after he had been discharged from hospital, Toby was driving to Abuja, having received calls from both Dare and his younger sister, Oiza, that urgently required him to travel. As Toby drove into Abuja town proper he veered off the main highway at the busy AYA Junction towards Asokoro, and he took a deep breath. He did not like Abuja much. Nothing save pressing business issues and family could make him come. And he was here for both reasons.

He turned off the main road leading to the ECOWAS Secretariat into a small street lined with trees and the mansions of the Abuja elite. The neighbourhood was quiet, with poplar trees lining the sides of the streets and large pavements made of interlocking tiles. Houses of varying sizes and architectural influences flanked the narrow tar road, with ubiquitous 'Beware: heavily guarded' signs posted on the imposing gates.

Soon enough he found the place he was looking for and he drove into the large parking lot where there were three expensive cars parked. Nothing is too good for the law firm of Mustapha, Bello and Obanye, he thought.

He stepped out of the car and walked into an expansive foyer, all glistening marble, chrome and leather. A pretty and efficient-looking secretary sat at a desk outside one of the three large doors. She looked up, her bored expression changing as she visibly brightened up at seeing Toby. He noticed her casting a quick glance at his left ring finger and, seeing it bare, flashed him a beautiful smile. Toby was bemused at her appraisal and smiled back blandly.

"Good afternoon, sir," she purred, her eyes fixed on him. "How may I help you?"

"I'd like to see Barrister Bala Mustapha, please," he said.

"He's in a meeting now. If you don't mind waiting I'll see if he would be able to see you, sir," she said with a coquettish smile on her face.

"That's fine," he said, sitting down in a comfortable leather chair. He took out his phone and made a quick call to his assistant in Jos to give him some instructions. When he hung up he found the secretary looking at him as if she were the shark in *Jaws* spotting a lone swimmer. He had no interest in flirting with anyone, no matter how attractive.

He sat there, deep in thought. No matter how he tried to fill his mind with matters pertaining to The Bar-Rage and even Oiza, other thoughts kept intruding. He remembered the last time he had seen Bala: a thoroughly unpleasant meeting. He supposed it couldn't be helped, considering the circumstances. He hadn't seen Bala in years and was unsure of the reception he would receive. But that was neither here nor there: he had a mission and he would fulfil it. He picked up a magazine from a nearby table and skimmed articles he wasn't really interested in.

Half an hour later he heard movements coming from the inner office and then a door creaked open. He looked up, as a man in a flowing babban riga came out. The man stopped and turned around, speaking Hausa and laughing at a response that came from inside the office. He was followed by another man. He looked exactly like Toby remembered. He was tall and dark with a dignified air, his tailored suit framing his powerfully built figure. He looked a lot like the British actor Idris Elba, with the same intense gaze and no-nonsense demeanour.

The man was Bala Mustapha: Toby's one-time close friend ... and Hannani's husband.

***

Bala Mustapha, the son of a wealthy oil magnate from Kebbi state, had an air of grandeur and entitlement about him, which Toby was quite familiar with. They had been friends since their NYSC days when Bala's arrogance had often been tempered by Toby's more mellow character. Toby had lost track of the number of times he had defused situations in which Bala's attitude could have landed them both into big trouble. Even Bala's father had advised him to keep Toby as a friend, commenting that he hoped some of Toby's temperance would rub off on his volatile son. Their friendship had worked well enough, mostly because Toby didn't allow Bala's flippant attitude to faze him. But it had all changed the day Toby had introduced Bala to Hannani.

Bala stopped cold when he saw Toby, his face registering shock, which he quickly replaced with a smile, as he resumed his discussion with the man in the babban riga. They both walked slowly towards the entrance, the man greeting Toby as he passed and Toby responding. When the visitor finally left, Bala turned to face Toby, his frame taut.

Toby stood up, his arms hanging loosely at his sides and they studied each other evenly. They were about the same height, though Bala was slightly bigger in build. The secretary looked at both men, uncertain of what to do. Bala addressed her without looking at her.

"Dumebi, you can go for your lunch break now."

"But sir, I've already gone for—"

"Go," he commanded, his tone clipped.

She stood up quickly, grabbed her bag and scuttled past Toby, her heels clacking loudly on the interlocking tiles in the courtyard. Bala turned his attention back to Toby.

"You really have liver," Bala said, narrowing his eyes. "You should know that you're the last person in this world I want to see."

"I have no doubt of that," Toby said calmly. "But I have something to discuss with you."

"I feel like choking you right now," Bala said, clenching his fists. Toby felt the hairs on the back of his neck rise and readied himself for a possible altercation, something he had hoped to avoid at all costs.

"You want to do that here?" Toby said, putting his hands in his pockets.

"Get out," Bala said. Toby didn't move, his jaw tightening. "Not until you hear what I have to say. And don't try and pull that self-righteous move on me: it won't work. We both know you're not the saint you'd like people to think you are," Toby said with a hint of warning in his voice.

Bala drew in a sharp breath and for a moment Toby saw his ice-cold veneer crack. It was clear that Bala understood the message behind Toby's words. Without saying another word, he walked towards his office and Toby followed him in.

As they walked in Toby felt his feet sinking into a lush carpet. There was an exquisite Turkish rug in the centre of the room, with a large cedarwood desk on it. A piece of jazz was playing softly, though he couldn't see where the speakers were. He could also hear the low hum of an air conditioner, also hidden from view. A quick glance around the office revealed Bala's superb and expensive taste, with beautiful framed artworks on the wall. Bala sat down in his chair behind the desk and Toby sat across from him. Bala brought his hands together in front of him, drumming his fingers, and gave Toby a piercing stare. Toby didn't flinch. There was a picture of Hannani and a little girl displayed prominently on the desk. Toby glanced at it but said nothing.

"Eh-hehn?" Bala said, impatience colouring his tone.

"I need you to win a case for me," Toby said. Bala shrugged, his expression unchanged.

"And so what does that have to do with me?"

"You're the best there is: you always win," Toby said.

"What makes you think I would do anything to help you?" Bala spat out the words. Toby calculated his words carefully, knowing from experience what would have the most impact on Bala.

"Because I've done the same for you more times than I can count, Bala," he replied. "Have you forgotten the many times I did damage control for you when you messed up? The times I stood by you when no-one else would? Your personal issues with me shouldn't cloud your judgement."

"You slept with her, Toby," Bala hissed, and for a moment Toby thought he would launch himself over the desk. "You slept with my wife."

"She was not your wife when that happened, Bala. And if I could take that back I would, I really would."

"You have no idea what it is to love a woman and know she's thinking about someone else all the time," Bala said, his voice low and pained.

"Actually, I do, Bala. Hannani married you, not me. She loves you, not me. I learned to live with that fact and I moved on."

"Moved on?" Bala said bitterly. "How convenient for you. It was just your usual 'hit-and-run', wasn't it?"

"It wasn't like that," Toby answered. "But then I'm not here to talk about Hannani. The past is the past. You've got your family and I've got my life. I've never asked you for anything before: now I am."

"I'm not doing anything for you," Bala said, his tone dismissive as he began to rise from his seat.

Toby didn't move. He hated the thought of what he would have to do to ensure Bala's cooperation, but it had to be done.

"How is Amina, by the way? And Bilqis?" Toby asked, looking squarely at Bala. The man froze in mid-rise. He seemed to turn several shades darker as a hunted look crossed his eyes, his mouth slightly open. Toby decided to increase the pressure a notch higher.

"You *do* remember them, don't you? They *are* your daughters after all. One in Lagos and the other in ... is it Warri?"

Bala closed his mouth and swallowed several times. He sank back into his seat. Toby knew then that he had him exactly where he wanted him.

"Have you forgotten I was the one whom you asked to help you ... 'settle' their mothers when you got them pregnant, abi? And this was around the time you and Hannani got engaged, wasn't it?" With each word Toby spoke, Bala looked more deflated. He went on.

"And Hannani heard rumours that you had cheated on her. But she didn't know about the children, did she? I'll bet she still doesn't know, Bala." Toby then rose and placed his palms on the table, leaning towards Bala slightly. Toby spoke slowly and deliberately, as though he were reciting poetry to Bala rather than reminding him of past indiscretions.

"And I didn't tell her then, Bala. As much as I wanted to, I knew that I didn't want Hannani to end up with me just because she was angry with you. So tell me: what's it like balancing three different families and trying to keep secrets from all of them?"

"Are you blackmailing me?" Bala asked, finally looking straight at Toby. He was spoiling for a fight, Toby could see, but he refused to take the bait.

"I'm trying to convince you to do something good for someone else – for once in your life, Bala," Toby said. "After this, you'll never see me again. I'll keep your little secrets. It's a simple bargain, I think."

"You're bluffing," Bala said, grasping at straws.

"Try me, Bala," Toby said with finality. "Unlike you, I have nothing to lose." In truth he had no intention of telling Hannani anything, even if Bala called his bluff and refused his request. He didn't have it in him to do it and he did not want to cause Hannani any more heartache.

The men looked at each other without flinching for what felt like many minutes. Then Bala looked away and put his hand to his mouth, as though he were in deep thought. When he looked back at Toby, he asked a single question.

"How soon does the case go to court?"

*** 

Adoo looked at her telephone screen, relief flooding over her as she read the text from someone she assumed to be Auntie Benita.

*Darling, I called the lawyer and you should be expecting a call anytime from now. Please let me know if ...*

The text was incomplete – but she had gotten the most important part of it. Auntie Benita, in her usual scatterbrained fashion, had listed her number as 'unknown'. She told Aduke about the text, wondering when she would hear from the lawyer.

Adoo didn't have the luxury of dwelling on her feelings as the lawyer called her that evening, insisting on meeting her the next day.

"Miss Ibi, I would like to have a meeting with you as soon as possible. How about tomorrow? The quicker we begin proceedings the better your chances," he said over the phone, his tone professional and curt. Adoo bit her lip as she held the phone, thinking about all the arrangements she had to make. After the phone call, she dashed to her room to begin packing and making calls to arrange transport and accommodation in Abuja.

In the frenzy of it all, she realised that she had not seen Toby since he had been discharged from the hospital. He had mentioned in a phone call a few days earlier that he had to make a quick trip out of town. He hadn't mentioned the destination or reason and she hadn't wanted to pry. The conversation had been rather short and had felt a little stilted. At least she had been pleased to find out that he was well enough to be discharged.

She had so many feelings to sort out but hadn't

thought a phone call was the right time to bring them up. As much as her heart ached for him, she would have to put a conversation about her feelings aside.

She tried to call Toby a few times after her meeting with the lawyer but the connection was bad. She sat and looked at the phone in frustration, wanting to toss it across the room. Her friend Chisom, in whose flat she was staying, was still at work and she needed to get out, feeling as though the walls were closing in on her. She decided to go to Amigo in Wuse 2 to buy some ice cream. She remembered enjoying it from her last trip to Abuja.

Soon enough she was in the taxi, digging into her cup of chocolate ice cream on her way to Chisom's. The driver decided to take a route that landed them smack in the middle of a go-slow at one of the busier junctions around Maitama.

The taxi edged slowly forward, along with all the other cars stuck in the flow and Adoo leaned back, resigned to waiting it out.

To pass time, Adoo looked around at the high-rise offices, banks and streets. Then she saw something that made her blood run cold.

In front of one of the banks, she saw Toby standing in a short queue at an ATM, with his arm around the shoulder of a woman. Adoo remained transfixed, unable to tear her eyes away from the scene. It was unmistakably him. She would know his profile anywhere, not to mention his build and laid-back demeanour.

The woman was talking to him, judging from the way he was staring down at her. The lady was slim and dark, with a perfectly coiffed pageboy hairstyle and a stylish azure shift dress that ended above her knees, her legs made even longer by her medium-heeled black shoes. She leaned in to him and he held her even closer as she looked up at his face. Adoo couldn't see his expression, but the woman was looking at him with an unmistakable expression of love.

Adoo couldn't take any more. She closed her eyes and sank low into her seat, hoping that Toby wouldn't spot her.

*So that was why he came to Abuja*, she thought. Pain filled her as the realisation washed over her that her feelings for Toby would not be reciprocated.

\*\*\*

"Toby, I really don't know how you can stand this heat," the slim, dark lady with striking features moaned. Toby turned to look at her, his irritation melting away.

"Oiza, you know very well that nothing would make me come out in this heat except money and family. And in this case it just happens to be both." His sister chuckled.

"Look, I'm really sorry for the short notice but I had to see you first before going to Mama and Papa. You know they wouldn't understand about me and Jamie …" she said, her voice trailing off.

"Does Jamie know you're here?"

She nodded. "I took a few days off work, but I need to be back in the States in three days. I just need you to talk to Mama and Papa before I go to see them myself."

Toby sighed. His younger sister had a way of getting herself into odd situations and had called him from the U.S. to help her out. They were very close and he found it hard to refuse her anything, including her request that he keep her visit to Nigeria between them. He had gone to pick her up at the airport and had stopped at an ATM before dropping her off at her hotel.

"They will come around once you make it clear that this is what you want and that you are sure about the whole thing," he said.

"I am."

"Then I'm with you all the way," Toby said, pulling her close to him as she put her arm around him, looking up at him lovingly.

"Thanks, big bro. But you'll call them first and ... well, soften the blow?" She widened her eyes at him, pleadingly, a look he knew well. He smiled and nodded. Then he turned to the ATM, relieved that it was finally his turn.

# Eleven

Toby called Adoo later that evening, while she was brooding over seeing him with that woman. She steeled herself, prepared to be cordial but not too open.

"Hi, Adoo, it's been a while … how are you?" he asked, as though they had been keeping in touch regularly.

"Fine," she answered flatly.

"Oh … that's good," he said. There was a moment of awkward silence before he went on. "Are you in Jos?"

"No, I'm in Abuja."

"Oh really? So am I. Where are you staying? Maybe I can swing by?"

As much as she wanted to yell at him and tell him to stay away from her, the desire to see him overruled her pragmatism. She gave him the address and, when Toby hung up, she thought about what she was going to say to him.

Half an hour later he called to let her know he was in the building parking lot. Chisom wasn't home from work yet and Adoo decided to meet Toby outside. She spotted his car, opened the door and slid in, feeling the familiar comfort roll over her. As she turned to face him she wanted to put her arms around his neck, and then she remembered how she had seen the other women draped over him earlier in the day. She stiffened as annoyance seeped in.

He put on the inside light and it cast a warm glow over his face. He turned to her and reached out to put his hand over hers, smiling.

"It's good to see you, Adoo."

"You too, Toby," she said unenthusiastically. She slowly pulled her hand away from his and placed it on her lap. He seemed to sense her distance and pulled back.

"How has your trip been so far? How long is it till the court case?"

'We're going to court in a few days, I hope." Then, before she could stop herself, she asked, her tone biting. "And how has *your* trip been?"

"Uhm … it's been OK." His hesitance before answering only sharpened her suspicion. *Oh, I'm sure it has*, she thought, jealousy cutting into her.

"That's good," she answered. She waited, hoping he would say something about the woman she had seen him with and put her mind at rest but she didn't want to be the one to bring it up; she wasn't about to play the wronged woman and make a spectacle of herself. There was silence for a few seconds before he responded.

"Well … OK then. I'm sure you'll win the case, Adoo."

"Amen to that, Toby."

The atmosphere in the car began to stifle Adoo and she had an overwhelming urge to leave, to escape into the safety of Chisom's flat and gather her frayed nerves. She felt that, with the level of friendship they had reached, he could have at least respected her enough to tell her that he was seeing someone.

"Uhm … I have to go now. I'm heading to Makurdi tomorrow and I need to get ready," she said.

Adoo noticed the slight crease that appeared between Toby's eyes and the twitch as he tightened his jaw, perhaps in response to the cold edge in her reply, she thought. She felt justified in her iciness.

"OK then, I won't keep you. Have a safe trip and good luck, Adoo." His voice seemed detached and Adoo took it in, understanding that something vital between them had changed. She nodded and stepped out of the car, forcing a closed smile on her face as she wished him a good night. She turned and heard him start the car, reverse and drive out. She didn't turn around.

\*\*\*

The Third District Magistrate's Court of Makurdi was stifling and humid, the heat made worse by the various body odours of a hundred different bodies. Adoo wondered if the courtroom was near an incinerator, as she could also detect the acrid stench of burning rubbish. The expansive room was sparsely furnished and decorated, with old linoleum worn through in some areas exposing the grey concrete floor. The high ceilings had cobwebs at the corners, and only two of the six fans suspended from the ceiling beams were working. Their creaking as they spun added to the steady hum of conversation from the people in the court, mostly from those seated adjacent to Adoo and her lawyer. There were simple pew-like benches on both sides of the room and an elevated podium at the front of the row where the magistrate was seated. A few bored-looking policemen lounged about the entrance and the sides of the room. She rubbed her sweaty palms on her hips, not worrying too much about the state of her Ankara outfit.

The heat didn't bother Adoo. She had just won the case for custody and it was all she could do not to leap and scream for joy.

She looked over at Teremun with a smug smile on her face. He gave her a sullen look before turning away. She then looked over at her lawyer and grinned.

Her lawyer turned to her and said, "I don't normally like travelling so late, but there's an important meeting in Abuja that I must attend tomorrow.

Adoo frowned. "You're going to risk the road and travel at this time?"

"This is one of the hazards of our profession," he shrugged, with a smile.

"OK then, the driver will take you to your hotel after dropping me at my parents."

"Good, my driver will be waiting for me," he said.

As they drove off Adoo leaned back and closed her eyes, remembering bits and pieces of her initial meeting with her lawyer and how it had all culminated in the dramatic scene that had just passed at the court.

Their first meeting had taken place in his plush office in Abuja. As they discussed the basics of her case she had noticed a picture of a pretty, light-skinned woman and a child on his desk, his wife and daughter, no doubt. Something about the woman made her intuition buzz with a sense of recognition, even though she knew they had never met. He did not mention them, so she didn't ask, but she immediately felt an unspoken kinship with him as a fellow parent.

"I'm curious, Barrister," she had said. "How did you hear of my case?"

She could have sworn his lips tightened a fraction but his expression remained blank. "A ... mutual friend spoke to me about it and I was interested in taking the case up." Adoo nodded, assuming Auntie Benita was the friend in question. When she had brought up the issue of payment he had shaken his head.

"That has been taken care of, Miss Ibi," he said in a tone that brooked no argument. She looked at him in confusion.

"But, sir, I insist ..." she started to say and once again he shook his head.

"There is no point in insisting, Miss Ibi. As I said earlier, it has been taken care of. Just concentrate on getting all the documents and yourself ready to appear in court," he said, a slow smile appearing on his face but not quite reaching his eyes. Had Auntie Benita paid the bill? Or perhaps he owed her a favour? Adoo had questions but one look at his closed expression made her reserve those until a more fitting time. She would make it a point to ask Auntie Benita once she could reach her.

A few days before Adoo was scheduled to appear in court the lawyer flew into Makurdi, ready to represent her. Adoo had arranged for him to be accommodated in the best hotel in town, with first class treatment.

Bala had immediately made contact with Teremun's lawyer and suggested a meeting at the lounge of the hotel he was staying in, hoping that Adoo and Teremun could come to some arrangement. Teremun had refused, insisting they would meet in court. Adoo had been beside herself with nerves.

The car slowed and Adoo snapped out of her daydream as they approached the massive gates to her family home.

The driver hooted and the gates swung open. She saw her mother standing on the porch, watching Zander as he ran around in the far end of the compound. She looked up expectantly. Adoo smiled in anticipation of narrating the full story to her family.

She had stayed with her parents for the few days before the court case, preferring the familiar environment of home to the impersonal coldness of a hotel room. Besides, she thought it would be a chance for her to try to patch things up with her parents in the process. After the court victory, she was confident that it would be a new era in the relationship between her and her family. Adoo smiled in anticipation of sharing the good news with her family.

As the car stopped she turned to the lawyer and thanked him effusively. He smiled and nodded, saying, "It's been a pleasure working for you, Adoo. I can't recall a more pleasant client. I wish you the very best in everything." She nodded and stepped out of the car.

Zander spotted her and shrieked, breaking into a full run towards her, his arms wide open and face wreathed in smiles.

Adoo's throat clogged up as she bent down and opened her arms, ready to catch her son and hold him tight. He crashed into her and she almost lost her balance as she held his warm little body, stroking his head and back. He pulled back, eyes wide and luminous.

"Mummy … you cry?" he said, his face creased in worry, as he wiped the tears she was unaware had run down her face.

"Yes, baby, I cry. I cry because I'm happy and I love you very much." He scrunched up his face in confusion and then shook his head. She laughed as she swung him up. Wow, he's getting heavier, she thought. She looked up at her mother, who had the soft, understanding look only a mother could.

"I think a celebration is in order, eh?" she said. "Who wants to go out for cake and ice-cream?" If Zander's delight could get any louder she was sure the neighbours would come running. Her grandmother and mother walked in, the object of their joy and affection nestled contentedly in Adoo's arms.

\*\*\*

Toby remained in Abuja until Oiza returned after seeing their parents in Lokoja. He was happy to hear that she had been able to have a good talk with them, after Toby had softened the blow. She had been full of enthusiasm as he saw her off at the airport. She hugged him tightly, declaring him to be the best brother in the world, before she boarded her flight. He smiled as he drove back to Abuja, his sister's happiness temporarily dulling the ache within him at the cold reception he had received from Adoo. He didn't think he would ever understand the woman. He wasn't even sure he had the energy to try.

He decided to focus on his meeting with Dare the next day, to discuss pressing legal issues pertaining to the business. That would take his mind off Adoo.

The meeting went on longer than planned and after they had finished he looked at his watch, realising that it was mid-afternoon and he hadn't eaten. He decided to stop at a popular eatery, Miss Dee's Pizza, and grab some lunch before heading out of Abuja to Jos.

Miss Dee's was not crowded, but there was a lot of noise coming from the children's play area, which he was in no mood for at the moment. Most of the patrons of the eatery were harried mothers trying to get a breather from their children who were running around and shrieking at the top of their lungs on the jungle gyms and play equipment next door. Toby scanned the area, looking for a quiet place to sit down. He spotted a vacant table near the corner, which he quickly took.

He had just settled down to eating his overpriced meal, when a shadow fell over him. He really didn't feel like sharing the table, so he didn't lift his head. A female voice spoke.

"Toby? Toby is that you?"

Shock ran through his body as memories flooded his mind: jumbled images, colours and sounds all coming together to form a vivid picture. His head snapped up as he looked at the woman in front of him.

"Hannani?"

# Twelve

She stood drilling holes into him with her earthy brown eyes rimmed with black kohl, their expressiveness unhindered by her rimless glasses. Her perfume swirled around him and reminded him of Arab coffee and incense. Her slicked-back hair was loosely covered with a diaphanous veil. Her beautifully embroidered Pakistani-style kaftan flowed over her frame, which seemed fuller than he remembered. She looked lovely.

"I see you haven't forgotten me," she drawled. Her voice was still as honeyed as ever. Sweet, she had been. He wondered what kind of cosmic coincidence had allowed him to avoid both Bala and Hannani for years and then be put him in a situation where he not only had to seek Bala out but then bumped into Hannani not too long after.

He looked at her evenly and asked, "How are you, Hannani?"

"I am ... fine," she said hesitantly, her tone guarded. "May I sit down?"

"Please, go ahead." She sat down across from him, loosely folding her exquisitely manicured hands resting lightly on the table. She had tasteful and expensive rings on both of her ring fingers. Everything about her suggested understated wealth and she carried it with poise and elegance.

"Now this is odd, running into you here of all times and places," Hannani said and inclined her head towards the play area. "I'm here with my daughter, Faiza. She wanted to play so I left her next door with the house help and came in here for a breather ... and look who I found."

He smiled, sipping on his drink, his appetite gone. He felt his guard coming up and thought it best to keep his answers as short as possible and let her direct the flow of conversation.

"Yes, it is unexpected, bumping into you here," he said.

"But you don't live in Abuja, do you?"

"No, I live in Jos."

"Oh, I see," she said and there was an uncomfortable silence between them.

"So ... are you married?" she finally asked.

"No," he said.

"Not yet, you mean," she said. "Well, whoever you marry will be a very lucky woman." He raised his brows, surprised at the compliment.

"Thank you," he answered, wondering where the conversation was heading. She nodded and he could see, from her rigid composure as she sat with her back totally straight, that she was uncomfortable. He attempted to alleviate the tension.

"The awkward factor is high, isn't it?"

She smiled before answering. "Maybe, but I'm actually glad I ran into you."

"Why?"

142

"Oh, I don't know. Maybe I feel better now seeing that you look so well, like you haven't been at all affected by … uhm." She glanced down at her lap briefly before looking back up, her face a mask of calm, concealing all previous signs of discomfort. "Or maybe I just want to talk and catch up."

"Catch up? On what exactly?" He hadn't intended to sound so blunt but it came out that way. He waited for the rush of desire to come, the raw need, but felt nothing. Only vague discomfort, as though he needed to get as far away from her as possible. He looked at Hannani and saw an unattainable woman and, strangely, he had no yearning to be with her at all. Falling in love with Adoo must have a lot to do with that.

She was quiet and Toby thought that perhaps she would get up and leave. Then she spoke again, her voice so low he almost missed her question.

"Toby, do you ever think of me?"

He hadn't expected that, hadn't thought she would delve into something so personal. Toby thought carefully about how to answer the question and decided not to lie or sugar-coat anything. If the reason for this chance meeting with Hannani now was to finally excise her from his life then he was prepared to do so.

"I used to think about you every day until quite recently, Hannani. And there were moments I thought I would never love another woman like I loved you at one time."

"And?"

"And I moved on. But you haven't answered my question Hannani … what do we have to talk about?"

"I don't really know. Maybe I miss you, and maybe I miss our friendship and … I don't know, maybe I'm sorry about what happened and how things turned out. I sometimes wonder 'what if'…"

There rose an edge to Hannani's voice; it was the same tone she had used when she had come to him all those years back. She sounded like someone trapped and reaching out to grasp a lifeline.

"It's a little too late for 'maybe' and 'what if', Hannani. And though I admit that I have also had moments where I have missed our friendship I know that it's not something that can work now." He spoke gently, taking care to keep any malicious edge out of his voice.

Hannani nodded and looked away, but not before he caught the sheen of tears in her eyes. He felt a wave of pity for her, for the woman he once loved. He'd never seen her look so dejected. Against his better judgement he asked her a question.

"Are you unhappy, Hannani?"

She looked back at him and, although the tears were gone, her eyes were watery. She looked weary. She sighed before speaking.

"Marriage isn't all I thought it would be, but in reality what is? Sometimes I think about what it would have been like if I had chosen another option rather than the one I did … if I had chosen you."

Toby tensed up. The conversation was taking a dangerous curve.

"Hannani, I want you to know something. You were once a part of my life, and a good part at that. I'm not going to pretend that the years of friendship we had before meant nothing to me. They did, and I have no regrets about those times."

"Neither do I, Toby," she countered, her eyes guarded.

"But our lives took different paths and I've come to accept it. We both paid our dues. What's the use of bringing up the past when it doesn't make the present better?"

"Look, Toby, I'm just … I guess seeing you after all these years just made me think things I shouldn't. We've made our choices. I made mine years ago and I'm sorry if you felt you paid for them, I really am."

He felt the tension leave him as he realised that both of them bore wounds, but his were the ones that had healed.

"It's OK, Hannani." They fell silent, Toby's mind drifting to the passing time and his trip back to Jos and Hannani biting her lip lightly, looking as though she had something to say but wasn't sure how to approach it. Finally she spoke.

"What's her name?"

"Who?" He was confused.

"The woman on your mind, Toby," she asked. The image of Adoo flashed into his mind. His defences dropped a little, and he relaxed as he answered.

"Her name is Adoo."

Hannani smiled, her tone measured as she spoke. "I'm sure she's fascinating."

"Small but mighty, I would say," Toby said. "She has a way of bringing sunshine into the lives of those she meets."

In those few seconds Toby realised just how much he loved and missed her: her smile and unique laugh, her wit, faith and infectious enthusiasm for life. He wondered why she had been so cold the last time that they'd spoken. But he figured she might have been tense because of the court case. He also knew that he had valid reasons for staying away from her during that time, all for her good.

He snapped back to reality and saw Hannani leaning back and looking at him as though studying him.

"It's obvious you love her very much, Toby. And I'm happy for you," she said. "Does she love you back?"

"I don't know," he answered.

"Then what are you waiting for? Why don't you find out?"

"It's not that simple," he said, putting his palms down on the table. Hannani shook her head and made a dismissive motion with her hand.

"Oh yes it is, Toby. It really is. Either she loves you or she doesn't."

"I'm rather surprised to hear this from you, Hannani."

She shrugged. "Life tends to drag the truth out of you whether you like it or not. I've had to learn some things the hard way. Look, Toby, you have a chance to find love.

146

So go and take it and hold on to it even if it means a fight. Don't get the wind knocked out of you before you try."

He looked at Hannani and caught a glimpse of the woman he had known and loved all those years ago, when their days were still filled with the innocence of true friendship.

He wanted to reach out to touch her hand, but the gesture could be misconstrued, so he didn't. She seemed to sense his withdrawal and she reciprocated, her expression hardening and her posture straightening. She exhaled, looking out towards the area where her daughter was playing.

"It's wonderful seeing you again, Toby," she said as she rose. "I have to go now." Standing, she shed the shell of the carefree friend and lover of the past and became once again Hajiya Hannani Mustapha. Toby nodded.

"Yes, it is," he said, rising to his feet and smiling at her. "I wish you the very best in life, Hannani. I really mean it." She returned the smile, her eyes a little sad.

"You too, Toby, and all the best with Adoo." She turned and walked out.

Standing there, Toby let out a breath, running through the entire conversation in his mind. As he left the building, a sense of freedom overwhelmed him. Driving out of Abuja towards Jos, he thought about Adoo. He would set out to win her over fully, with Zander in the picture, and he would give her the very best of himself, with no holds barred.

Auntie Benita called a week after the court appearance and a day before Adoo was to return to Jos. She had already packed and was lying down in her room, trying to nap when the phone rang.

"Eh, DooDoo, I hear you came out of the battle victorious," Auntie Benita said with a flourish. Adoo chuckled.

"I did, Auntie, and I owe you thanks for that," she said.

"Yes, Mercy is a good lawyer, isn't she?" Auntie Benita said. Adoo shook her head in confusion.

"Auntie, who is Mercy?"

"Barrister Mercy Eke-Folarin. I called her and asked her to get back to you. I assume she handled your case?" Aunty Benita sounded perturbed, adding to Adoo's sense of bewilderment.

"Auntie, the lawyer who handled my case was Barrister Bala Mustapha of Mustapha, Bello and Obanye Chambers in Abuja," Adoo said slowly.

"Oh my ..." Auntie Benita said. Then, as if remembering something, she huffed. "Oh my word. Oh dear."

"What is it, Auntie?" Adoo asked, alarmed.

"I called Mercy the day before I travelled and told her about your case, but I didn't give her your number. I told her I would send a text but ... I don't think I ever did. There was no way she could have got hold of you. I am so sorry, my dear."

Adoo's mind was already too jumbled. She couldn't

also worry about this. She mumbled something, reassuring her Auntie that she was not offended. She had won the case and that was all that mattered.

Adoo ended the call; her mind racing with questions. *If Auntie had not arranged for Bala Mustapha to handle her case, then who had?*

As soon as she got off the phone with Auntie Benita, she called Bala Mustapha. When she got him on the phone, after the appropriate greetings, she went straight to the point.

"Barrister, when you referred to a mutual friend that spoke to you about my case I was under the impression that the 'friend' in question was my aunt, Barrister Benita Oyebade. It seems I was mistaken."

He didn't respond so she pressed on. "Please … if Auntie Benita didn't make the connection then who did?"

He remained silent for a bit before clearing his throat, making Adoo wonder why he was delaying replying. Did he have something to hide?

"Let's just say I repaid a debt I owed someone by taking your case," he said, his voice taking on a tone that made her think he wanted to avoid answering directly. *Debt? An enigma if anything.*

"Really? Could you tell me who that is?" she asked. At that moment she heard a woman's voice and the sound of a child shrieking. She heard muffled voices, as though he were talking to someone.

"I really must go now, Adoo. Take care of yourself and your son," he said hurriedly before hanging up.

Adoo held her phone for a few moments and then shrugged, deciding to let the issue drop. After all, however the connection to Barrister Bala Mustapha had come about in the end she had won the case. There was no need to rock the boat.

***

Adoo and Zander got back to Jos the following day tired and hungry. Aduke was obviously out: her car wasn't there and there were no lights on in the house despite the creeping darkness. Adoo dragged in their travelling bags and put on the generator while Zander whined in the background. She scanned the contents of the fridge and was relieved to find some bean porridge in a pot, which she quickly warmed up on the stove and gave to Zander. At that moment Aduke arrived and there was a flurry of hugs and greetings as she rushed in to drop her bags.

A little over an hour later, with Zander fed, bathed and asleep, Adoo and Aduke sat in the living room eating dinner as Adoo recounted the events of the past weeks, deliberately leaving out anything that involved Toby. She didn't think she was ready to delve into that matter knowing that Aduke would be very thorough in wanting to know the details. She would tell her about it when the time was right.

"Have you called this Barrister Bala Mustapha to ask who exactly connected him to you?" Aduke asked.

"I did but he was very vague. He said something about

paying a debt to a mysterious 'someone'," Adoo replied, leaning back, her food seemingly forgotten. "He didn't seem eager to discuss it. And I decided not to push the issue."

Aduke then put her fork down and leaned in. "So ... what about Toby? Did you hear from him?" *She certainly doesn't waste any time,* Adoo thought. *Well, I might as well spill it.*

Adoo shook her head. "Aduke, I saw him in Abuja after I had met the lawyer."

"And?" Aduke's eyes widened in interest. Adoo shook her head sadly.

"I saw him with a woman at an ATM. They had their arms wrapped around each other and it was obvious that ... well, he didn't see me anyway. I was inside a taxi."

Aduke's brow furrowed. "What? Are you sure it was Toby you saw?"

"Aduke, I'm sure," she answered. "And then later that evening, he came to see me and he didn't say anything about her."

"Maybe you misunderstood ..."

Adoo shook her head. "Believe me I didn't misunderstand anything, Aduke. Anyway, as much as it hurts, it's not like we were ever really a ... steady couple. I just wish he had told me about her."

"But you really like him, don't you?" Aduke's voice was full of understanding.

"I more than like him. I think I've fallen in love with

him. But time will change that. At least I hope so. I don't think we're meant to be." Adoo struggled to hold the tears back as she forced a smile. "Besides, the most important thing is that now I have full custody of Zander. Life will go on."

She got up and began to clear the table. Aduke looked like she wanted to say something but then thought better of it. Adoo walked into the kitchen and gave in to the silent tears that splashed into the sink as she rinsed the dishes.

*** 

A few days later as Adoo was driving home after Sunday service, Aduke asked her to stop so that she could buy *Panache*, a popular glossy magazine, from a newspaper vendor. Zander was singing a Sunday school song at the top of his lungs and Adoo's only wish at that moment was to get home as fast as possible. She reluctantly agreed and they stopped.

"I really don't know why you waste your time and money on that stuff," Adoo chided, heading back home as Aduke began to flip through the pages. "What's the point of looking at all those so-called celebrities attending parties?"

"Abeg, leave me, jor," Aduke said. "I like the fashion and make-up tips. And, I also happen to like the gist." Adoo hissed and shook her head.

When they got home Adoo went straight to the kitchen to prepare lunch while Zander played with some of his toys in the living room, making a racket in the process. Aduke sat in the living room, still flipping through the magazine.

Adoo had just begun to chop the vegetables when she heard Aduke call out from the living room. "Adoo, didn't you say your lawyer's name was Bala Mustapha?"

"Yes," Adoo shouted from the kitchen. "Why do you ask?"

"Because I'm looking at him right now in the magazine. Hah! The guy is so fine," Aduke said. Adoo rinsed her hands and walked into the living room. Aduke handed her the glossy, pointing to a picture.

Adoo found herself looking at her lawyer, Bala Mustapha. He was extremely dashing in a crisp blue kaftan, with his arm lightly resting on the shoulder of a caramel-skinned woman dressed in a sparkly, flowing pink jellabiya with a silky veil tossed over her head. The woman had glasses on, with her make-up impeccably applied on her smooth face. Her hair had been pulled back with a small widow's peak at the centre, revealing a round face with kohl-rimmed wide, bright eyes and a diminutive mouth. Adoo noticed that, aside from their eyes, she and the lady bore striking similarities in stature, form and even some facial features.

The caption under the picture read: Barrister Bala Mustapha and his lovely wife, Hajiya Hannani Mustapha, attend the grand opening of the new Children's Medical Centre in Maitama, Abuja.

Adoo blinked a few times trying to connect the dots. Hannani was not a common enough name for this lady not to be the very same one Toby spoke of. Slowly, realisation began to dawn as she fitted the pieces together.

Adoo put the magazine down and sank into her chair. It made sense now: Toby must have been the one who arranged their meeting. That also meant that he had taken care of the expenses. But why would Toby go to all that trouble? What did he stand to gain?

She needed answers. She picked up her phone and tried to call him, but a mechanical voice on the other end told her his number was unreachable. She looked up at Aduke who had a questioning expression.

"I need to see Toby."

"Maybe you can try and see him at The Bar-Rage this evening," Aduke suggested.

\*\*\*

"What do you mean he's not around? Then where is he?" Adoo asked, trying to rein in her temper. She was face to face with the surly hostess, Emem, again. This time it was evident that Emem was thoroughly enjoying the opportunity she had to infuriate Adoo by withholding information.

"Eh, I don't know when he'll be back," she said with a smug look on her beautiful face. "Shey, you have his number? Why don't you find out by yourself?"

"I've tried his number and I can't get through," Adoo replied. Emem shrugged.

"Well then, maybe he changed his number for some reason. Maybe you know what the reason is. All I know is that he's gone and I can't say more," she said, flouncing away and leaving Adoo standing and wondering where Toby had disappeared to.

# Thirteen

Toby's trip to Lagos had been unexpected. He had to supervise purchases for the new club Dare wanted to open in Kaduna. Dare insisted that only he was experienced enough and had the knowledge to handle matters.

He thought about calling Adoo the night before he travelled but changed his mind. He would speak to her face to face when he returned to Jos and tell her how he felt. He had some extra cash and decided that he would surprise Adoo by getting her some baking and decorating equipment and perhaps even pick up a toy or two for Zander. If he was going to tell the woman he loved her then it wouldn't hurt to go bearing gifts.

The flight to Lagos was stressful. First of all, the plane departed two hours later than scheduled and, by the time they landed in Lagos, the heat was at full blast. The airline had mixed up his luggage and it was another hour before he finally got his little travelling bag.

It was already 4pm and the domestic terminal of the airport was loud and bustling. Toby cursed under his breath as he tried to navigate his way out of the terminal, carrying his laptop case in one hand and his travelling bag in the other, while being bumped by people on all sides. On his way out of the airport doors, a wiry tout almost knocked him over.

"Oga, sorry o, no vex," the fellow said. Toby hissed

under his breath and continued out of the terminal. Outside, he hailed a taxi and quickly climbed into it. Soon they were on the highway headed to Ikoyi where he would be staying with Dare's brother.

In the taxi, he reached into his pocket for his phone. It wasn't there. He sat up and dug in all his pockets; both his phone and wallet were missing. His pockets had been picked, most likely by the tout who had bumped into him. He uttered a curse and leaned back against the seat, closing his eyes in frustration.

He would have to go to the bank to cancel his ATM cards immediately and report his missing driver's licence to the police. He would also have to go to his mobile service provider and have his SIM card replaced. All that would take an entire day to do in Lagos. He cursed again. Luckily, most of his cash was in his shirt pocket and laptop bag.

What bothered him most was the loss of his phone. He had all his contacts in there and the only backup copy of all his information was on an external hard drive, sitting in his bedroom back in Jos. He kept his most important numbers on speed dial, never bothering to memorise any.

He muttered under his breath about how he wanted to strangle a few people and the driver looked back at him through the rear-view mirror, obviously worried about the crazy passenger he had picked up.

It took another hour and a half to get to his destination. He paid the driver, walked up four flights of stairs until he reached the flat and knocked the door. Thankfully, Dayo was in.

"Ah, Bros! You dey so? Why you no call me? I didn't even know you landed," Dayo said, smiling as he opened the door to Toby, who looked worse for wear.

"It's a long story, Dayo … one I will tell you after I have had a bath and eaten something, when I'm feeling like a human being again," Toby said wearily as they walked into the flat.

*** 

He had been so busy for the past two weeks that he hardly had time to himself. Toby had forgotten just how hectic it could get in Lagos when one was trying to make purchases at opposite ends of town as well as take care of bank, phone and police issues at the same time. What he thought would take a day to achieve had taken him the better part of four days and so he ended up having to extend the trip in order to fit his official itinerary with his personal one. He had met up with lawyers representing Dare's company and it had taken several days for them to sort out the issues surrounding the company.

He had also got a new phone and a temporary SIM card and had tried to call Adoo several times, relying on his memory, but the calls kept disconnecting. He wondered if she had changed her number and, unfortunately, he had never got Aduke's number either so there was virtually no way for them to communicate.

Then it occurred to him that he had opened a Facebook account and he decided to see if he could find her there ... until he realised that he had forgotten his password and secret question. He seethed with frustration, wondering how on earth everything seemed to conspire to keep him from communicating with her.

*What if, she just doesn't want to hear from me? Or perhaps, she just needed space to process things,* he thought in the haze of his unhappiness and frustration.

He decided that, as soon as he returned to Jos, he would go and see Adoo and try to sort things out with her. The worst that could happen was that she would refuse to see him. But he resolved that when he finally saw her, he would not go empty handed. He was old-fashioned; he believed in lavishing gifts on the woman he cared about.

He'd visited two warehouses and a few stores including a large cake and confectionery one, trying to find what he was looking for. His head reeling from the bewildering array of products he'd seen, in the end he had begged Dayo's girlfriend, Bunmi, to go with him to help buy the 'chandelier crystal stand thing'. He remembered Adoo mentioning that particular item, along with some others he had forgotten. He asked Bunmi to use her discretion in picking other items.

He almost wept with joy when they finally found the crystal chandelier cake stand ... and then nearly choked when he was presented with the bill for what he thought amounted to a few pieces of strangely shaped plastic, silicone and aluminium. But he was assured that he had picked the best. Getting toys had been equally excruciating because he had no idea what kids of Zander's age liked. In the end, he picked the toys with the flashiest colours and knobs. *All for the love, my guy, it's all for love,* was the mantra he had to keep repeating to himself as he moved from one aisle to the next.

When he got to the airport he monitored his belongings closely and warned off a threat to a suspicious-looking character that came too close to him, ostensibly to offer his 'help' in carrying the load.

"If you no commot for road you go see wetin I go do you," he growled and the guy backed up in fright, his eyes wide as he retreated with mumbled apologies. Toby was in no mood to be robbed again.

Darkness had fallen as Toby sped along on his way to Rantya. He rehearsed what he would say to Adoo, saying the words aloud to himself.

*Adoo, I think we should take this thing to the next level ... Adoo, I think that you and I should ... we could make this relationship work out for ... we could ... I would like us to see if this could last. Let's both let go of our past and look to the future. Adoo, I love you.* Nothing seemed right, except for last sentence.

As he approached Adoo's gate he was exhilarated and at the same time nervous. Seeing her was something he needed to do, and rejection was not an option for him. He wasn't going to let her slip out of his grasp easily. She was worth fighting for. The guard let him in without a fuss. In a moment, he was knocking on her door. Aduke opened it and she gasped in surprise.

"It is you," she said.

"Er … yes, I am. Is Adoo in?"

"Aduke, who is it?" He heard her voice and knew then and there that he was where he belonged at last. Aduke stepped aside without a word and he went in.

\*\*\*

Adoo was standing at the far end of the living room in a pair of sweat pants and a huge Hello Kitty T-shirt that had seen better days. She squinted as she reached to put her glasses on. Her hair was piled into a messy ponytail and she was wearing a pair of fluffy slippers. When she saw Toby standing by the door she felt the telltale signs of tears coming on. She wasn't sure if the tears were from the sight of him or the fact that he had caught her in her ridiculous get-up. Aduke slipped into her room, closing the door quietly behind her.

Adoo and Toby stood and stared at each other for a moment before she spoke.

"I hate you," she said, even though she knew she was lying. She didn't hate him at all; she wanted to run across the room and throw her arms around him and hold him close. She needed every ounce of her willpower to stand still.

He took a step forward, but she held up a finger, halting

him where he stood. "Where have you been? I have been worried sick about you! You didn't call and I couldn't reach you. I thought you had been kidnapped or killed or gone and eloped with your Abuja girlfriend!"

"Abuja girlfriend?" he asked, his brow furrowed. "What are you talking about?" Adoo thought either he was a very good liar or he had a terrible memory and she proceeded to make things clear.

She crossed her arms, narrowing her eyes at him. "Oh, so you want to pretend you don't know? I saw you in Abuja, Toby. I saw you at that ATM, holding that woman. And even though you saw me later that evening I can't believe you wouldn't tell me you had someone else in your life."

Toby shook his head, his face still registering confusion. And then something like realisation began to cross his features. And he began to laugh. Adoo couldn't believe it! He was laughing? She could have happily punched him right then and there.

"Happy to see you find this funny," she hissed.

Toby continued to smile as he spoke. "The woman you saw me with, was she a dark, pretty woman of medium height?"

Adoo nodded, indignation filling her. Toby continued to speak, his tone one that could be used on a small child. "Adoo, that was my younger sister, Oiza. I had just picked her up from the airport and we had to stop at an ATM."

Adoo felt as though she had been punched in the gut,

totally winded. And she felt foolish for her assumptions.

"Oh," was all she could say in response.

"Jumping to conclusions can be a bit—"

"Don't say it."

He chuckled. "So ... all this was just a misunderstanding then. Are we cool?" he asked, holding his hands up in a gesture of surrender. "Uh ... I brought you cake stuff." Adoo's eyes widened in surprise.

Cake stuff? She felt the annoyance rise again: he had still disappeared for two weeks just like that and not bothered to contact her.

"You got me cake stuff? You disappear without a trace for the better part of a month and all you can say is 'I got you cake stuff'?"

"My phone and wallet were stolen when I landed in Lagos. I tried calling you but I couldn't get through. I swear, I did!" he insisted. "Isn't your number ..." he proceeded to rattle out the phone number.

Adoo nodded slowly. "Uh huh. Except that the last three digits are 931 and not 319, Toby." It all began to make sense to her and she felt her defences weaken.

Toby looked sheepish. "I know it's a lousy excuse but it's true. And I wasn't gone for a month. I was only gone for…"

"Thirteen and a half days, Toby," Adoo spoke softly, the fight gone from her. She had nothing left except the fact that, through it all, she still loved the man who stood in front of her.

"Yeah," he said dumbly.

"Why didn't you tell me about Bala?" Adoo asked.
Toby sighed.

"He didn't want me near him or you during the case.
He said he would drop the case if I didn't stay away. That,
coupled with the fact that I had already had a … er …
run-in with Teremun made me keep my distance. I wish I
hadn't. Believe me, Adoo, I wanted to see you so badly."
Each word made her warm up a little more to him.

"So you went to see him and told him about me?"

Toby put his hands in his pockets and nodded slowly,
his eyes never leaving Adoo's. She looked away, not
wanting to melt right before his eyes.

Adoo fell silent. Toby stood, as though didn't know
what to do.

"But why?" she asked. "Why would you go to all that
trouble, Toby? I don't understand."

"Isn't it obvious?" he asked, his expression open and
his voice soft. Adoo's arms hung loosely by her sides and
she felt hope rise in her as she listened. She knew exactly
what she wanted to hear from him. But he didn't bother
talking.

He took a few steps forward, pulled her into his arms
and held her close, breathing in deeply. "I came in from
Lagos today, just a little over an hour ago. You are the
very first person I have come to see. You, Adoo, in your
ridiculous T-shirt and fluffy slippers. Why would I do
that if I didn't love you?"

A feeling of warmth flowed through Adoo and she felt the tension leave her body. He loved her. Then a thought crossed her mind and she pulled back and looked at him, eyes wide and questioning. She noticed him stiffen and a look of worry crossed his face.

"And my pikin?" she asked, squinting up at him. He relaxed and smiled.

"I happen to like your pikin very much. I really hope all this toasting I'm doing is working because I come bearing gifts from afar, including that crystal stand thing you said you wanted. If you refuse my gift, I don't know if I'll be able to get a refund," he said, in mock seriousness. Adoo grinned as she leaned in to him, tipping her head back. He had actually remembered what she said she wanted from a conversation she could hardly even recall. She felt her heart swell at his consideration and thoughtfulness.

Adoo crinkled her nose. "Ehn? So now you're trying to bribe me with 'gifts from afar', abi? You are a true Nigerian." She put her hands on his chest and looked straight into his eyes.

"I think I love you too," she said, watching him as a slow grin spread across his face.

"Oh, you think?"

"I have loved you for a very long time, Toby, but I didn't want to let you know. I was afraid you would want to use me and that when you got tired you would dump me." She buried her face in his chest, wrapping her arms around him, relieved to finally be able to tell him how she truly felt. He rested his chin on her head and enveloped her in his arms.

"So, I guess we have to declare ourselves to Master Zander, abi?" Adoo said, as she brought her head up to look at Toby. He looked down at her with eyes filled with tenderness.

"Yes, nah. And if that doesn't work I can always worm my way into his heart with the help of Ben10 and company. Just the same way I've done with you." She nodded towards the door.

"Did you really bring me a lot of cake stuff?"

"Oh yeah. I have a feeling you might need some practice in making wedding cakes," he whispered.

Relief and contentment flooded Adoo as she held on to the man she loved and cherished. She reached up to pull his head down for a kiss, sighing as their lips met.

**ANKARA PRESS**
A New Kind of Romance

We hope you enjoyed reading this book. It was brought to you by Ankara Press, an imprint of Cassava Republic Press. The more you support us, the more contemporary African romance goodness we can produce for you. Here's how you can help:

**1. Recommend it**
Don't keep the enjoyment of this book to yourself; tell everyone you know. Spread the word to your friends and family.

**2. Join the conversation**
With Twitter, Facebook, blogs and even our own website, writing a review of a book you love has never been so easy. Start a conversation about the book via your own social networking site, or discuss it with others on Goodreads.com. And don't forget to leave a comment on www.ankarapress.com.

**3. Buy your own copy**
Encourage your friends to buy their own copy directly from our website (rather than illegally downloading it) as copies are available with special deals and discounts for them to enjoy. Your direct purchase will enable us to continue to produce the steamy stories you just can't get enough of. Support the publishers, not the pirates!

**4. Read our other racy romances**
We've more where this book came from and we promise that you won't be disappointed. In fact, we know that you'll be excited at having discovered our books. Browse and buy at www.ankarapress.com.

**5. Consider writing your own**
Have you ever thought about writing? Do you think you can compose a compelling African romance that will leave the reader hungry for more?

Then consider becoming one of our romance writers. Just follow our submission guidelines on www.ankarapress.com. We look forward to hearing from you!

Lastly, follow us on Twitter: @ankarapress, and like us on Facebook: www.facebook.com/ankarapressbooks.

## www.ankarapress.com

## About Sifa Asani Gowon

Sifa, a self-proclaimed sappy romantic soul, enjoys writing love stories almost as much as she enjoys reading them ... and she adores baking! She lives with her family in the city of Jos, a place of spectacular beauty, pleasant weather and the best vegetables you can find in Nigeria. *A Taste of Love* is her first novel with Ankara Press.

# If you enjoyed this, you'll definitely enjoy these: